JUST JENIFER

JUST JENIFER

BY

JANET LAMBERT

Jacket and Title Page Decoration by
ROBERTA PAFLIN

E. P. DUTTON & COMPANY, INC. · NEW YORK
1945

AMERICAN BOOK–STRATFORD PRESS, INC., NEW YORK

TO MARTY

JUST JENIFER

JUST JENIFER

CHAPTER I

OH, BEAUTIFUL day, Jenifer thought, not minding at all that a temperamental sky had burst into tears. She was comfortably ensconced in the living-room window seat, and with her back against a wall and her knees bent to make a bookrest she formed a contented letter N.

Her eyes were the color of the sky and the rain and she let them go racing back and forth across the pages of a magazine, while her hair, as bright as a winter oak leaf, hung like a protecting curtain between her and the world. Now and then she reached into a bag beside her for a cooky, chewed rhythmically, and dusted crumbs from her chest or her chin, and when she reached the last line of her story she brushed back her hair and leaned her head against the wall, prepared to chuckle over the words she had read. But shouts and running feet above her made her cast her eyes to the ceiling and she hung her magazine over her knees and sighed.

"I feel just like the old woman who lived in the shoe!" she told the ceiling grimly, "only I'll bet she didn't have to take care of her children when she was only sixteen years old with a war on." For some reason the idea amused her. She liked the thought of herself in a shoe with a lot of younger brothers and sisters, and in order to enjoy it she cupped her mouth with her hands and shouted upward:

"Hey, less noise up there. I'm thinking."

Semi-quiet answered her and she was about to settle back into her nest when she heard footsteps in the hall. She snatched up her magazine, bent her head again, and with her eyes as motionless as twin bird dogs on the point, held her breath while she listened.

"Hey, Jen!"

The voice was a deep croak in the hall and she hoped a high wing-back chair would hide the window seat, but her hopes were in vain.

"Jen?"

The voice came from inside the room this time and the click of a metal heeltap against wood told her its owner was lounging in the door, prepared to wait.

"All right," she said unwillingly, knowing she was caught. "What's wrong?"

"The kids. They want to know if you'll play 'orphan asylum' with them."

"Oh, Peter!" Jenifer scowled at the boy in the door. He had the same gray eyes, the same straight nose and full-curved mouth; but his forehead, broad and high like hers, was topped by a wheat-like stubble. "Do they *have* to be entertained?" she groaned.

"Well, they can't go outdoors and the playroom looks like heck and even the twins have had a fight."

"Oh. . . ." Jenifer closed her magazine reluctantly, as if to make sure none of the precious words escaped, before she looked up. "Will you play too?" she asked.

"Aw, I guess so." Peter pulled a hand from a pocket in his baggy cords and ran it through his wheat stubble without leaving a trace. "I kind of thought I'd work on my airplane," he muttered, "but nuts!"

"Well, of course it is awful out." Jenifer turned to look through the window at the sandy yard where harried grass was trying to amount to something. "You can't count on Florida weather in January," she murmured thoughtfully, "but I do think Mrs. Sanders should be more help to us on Rosie's day off. She cried all over her apron when Daddy was ordered overseas and said, 'Oh, General Jordon, I'll be a mother to your little darlings.' And is she? Pooh."

Jenifer swung her feet to the floor and sat kicking her sturdy saddle shoes against the window seat. "Where'd the old dragon go this afternoon?" she asked.

"She went to market I guess." Peter ran his hand through his hair again and Jenifer frowned at him.

"You're going to wear out the top of your head," she scolded. "I wish you'd never heard of a crew haircut." And then she continued equably, "I'll bet the dragon's riding around and using up all the gas. And she didn't even take Bitsy with her. She could at *least* have taken Bitsy."

"Bitsy wouldn't go. She yelled."

"Oh." Jenifer got up and shook herself more comfortably into her clothes. She smoothed the skirt of her green gingham and said, "We might as well get this over, so go out and call the mob."

"Okay."

But after Peter had gone she sat down again. With her legs stretched stiffly before her she studied the tips of her shoes and returned to her musing. She thought she had a better system than the old woman in the shoe because she gave more time to it.

Jenifer had been five when her mother died, leaving her to watch over a four-year-old Peter. She and Peter were proud of being called "army brats" and living in the small world of an army post. And then, when she was eight, her father had married again. That was when she really began to acquire her children. And while she had adored her sweet new ready-made mother, she had looked doubtfully at the two ready-made sisters who came with her. Gwenn and Alice were a little younger than Peter, and Jenifer started in early to train them.

"Listen," she said, standing in front of them and scowling, when they had been on the post a few days, "Peter and I are army. You two aren't anything."

The little girls who faced her sagged unhappily at this announcement for they had enjoyed their brief acquaintance with flags and bugles. "You're just civilians," Jenifer said. And then she relented. "I'll tell you what I'll do," she decided thoughtfully, "I'll let you be half-army. If you're good, that is, and mind me."

And when she was ten the twins were born. She sat in a big chair and held them, very carefully, one in each arm, rubbing her cheek against first one downy head and then the other. "They're army brats all right," she whispered triumphantly. "Neal's already yelling orders; and look, Susan's trying to salute us."

After the twins came Vance, then Bitsy. Seven little soldiers that now belonged only to Jenifer because another loving mother had to leave them in her care.

And as if they weren't enough she had inherited Donny.

General Jordon was packing to go overseas when the telegram about Donny came. The house was in a hullabaloo, with little Jordons tugging at trunk lockers and running with laundry or to the cleaners or trying out the new field glasses. "What under the sun will I do?" her father said, sitting down on the front steps and staring at the telegram.

Jenifer, beside him, tucked her arm through his and read the message again. "Regret to notify you," it said, "that your brother and his wife were killed in motor accident today. Please advise as to arrangements and the future of their son Donald." It was signed by a doctor, and Jenifer laid her cheek against her father's shoulder and said, "Donny can come here. He's ten and can take care of himself pretty well; he won't be any trouble."

So Donny slipped in between Alice who was a hoydenish twelve, and the twins who were six; and because he was a sweet, shy little boy it seemed as if he had always been there.

"Poor Donny," Jenifer would say, pitying him not so much for the loss of his parents as because he had entered the army so late in life. "Living here in Orlando with us, with Daddy away, and having no real army life, is a bad start for you. But you'll just have to muddle along until you can go to West Point."

Jenifer never doubted that all the boys would go to West Point and all the girls would marry officers. That was what one did in the army. And that was the way she trained them, loving them, and being tenderly patient.

It was unmilitary (all the children knew it and none dared admit it) but Jenifer's arms around them and her warm cheek pressed against theirs and her soft voice banishing their unsoldierly fears meant more to them than all the flags flying from all the flagpoles, or the bugles or reviews, or all the glory of fighting men. Sometimes they became tired of being so stoically army and wanted just Jenifer and the gay foolish things she did.

When that happened, now that their father was in Italy and they were living in Orlando for the duration of the war, she might become Ophelia, running about the lawn and talking madly to the flowers; not minding that pruning shears had stopped and rakes were as idle as her own lawnmower. Jenifer could bake a cake, reciting while she measured, "roll on, thou deep and dark blue ocean, roll," until the smallest Jordon shivered even in the heat of Florida.

And bedtime prayers weren't mumbled words to Jenifer; they were talking and being with God. And buttons hopped through hoops instead of being buttoned; and she called medicine ambrosia. And then there were the games she made up—games like "orphan asylum."

So they hung over the banister in the upstairs hall until Peter lounged against the newel post and beckoned to them. "Wahoo!" they shouted and descended in a rush. Flying figures slid down the well-polished rail, passing others that were leaping from step to step and leaving behind one small girl who was managing carefully.

Jenifer heard them coming and allowed herself a hearty sigh before she dashed to her father's desk that faced the long room. She took a pair of lensless glasses from a drawer, bobby-pinned her hair into a knot, and perched the glasses on her nose. Her stage was set.

"You may come in, children," she called, prim and scribbling on a scratch pad.

Only giggles answered her, followed by Peter's warning growl, then silence.

"Children, I said come in." Her voice was a prissy imitation of one of her teachers, for she was enjoying her game now as she enjoyed everything she did, and she leaned forward to watch the parade that came filing in led by Peter's tall fifteen and ending with Bitsy in a hop and a skip on the end. "Say 'Good afternoon, Miss Jordon,'" she prompted.

"Good afternoon, Miss Jordon."

Seven earnest faces were turned in a battery of floodlights on the desk and only Peter stood like a stork before the mantel, one foot hooked comfortably over an andiron. For all his seeming boredom he was ready to pounce if needed, but while Jenifer delivered her opening lecture he let his thoughts dwell on his half-completed plane.

"And so," Jenifer concluded, being thoroughly Miss Jordon now, "while I hate to have you leave our little nest, I have been able to secure lovely homes for you. Unfortunately, as you know, our superintendent is away. He. . . ."

"Do you mean Daddy?" a small voice piped.

"Our superintendent is away." Jenifer's gaze swept along the line, spinning out the thin thread of illusion that had almost snapped, until it rested on the unfortunate owner of the voice. "He has gone to war, Susan," she explained patiently, causing two round blue eyes to drop in shamed inspection of a rumpled pinafore, "as soldiers must."

"Yes'm." Susan's tan pigtails stood out from her bent head like ear trumpets and from force of habit she groped for a comforting hand. Neal thrust his out to her as a loyal prop from his half of the twinship, and they clung together.

Looking at them over her glasses, Jenifer pitied them; two solemn little first-graders who played a game too earnestly. So she smiled at them and scribbled on a piece of paper. "I've found a lovely home for you," she said briskly. "Here's the address and I know you'll be very happy there. Come, take it."

She held out the paper and watched them walk slowly forward and lift their hands as if receiving the Holy Grail; then she waved them to the door and turned her gaze on Gwenn.

Gwenn had struck a pose. She stood on patent leather toes, her head dramatically thrown back as if braced against a raging wind. Her teeth were bared to the gale, her eyes were shining sapphires and she looked like a tortured cover girl.

"Gwenn, stop it," Jenifer said, trying not to laugh. "I've got a place for you with a dancing teacher."

"Oh, Miss Jordon, rahlly? How too, too divine." Gwenn fluffed her yellow curls, gave a comic jerk to her neck and her knee that disrupted the admiring line, and went off around the room in a series of twirls.

"Could I go with her, Miss Jordon?" Alice asked, standing pigeon-toed and watching Gwenn who by now was leaning on the desk and lightly tapping the back of her head with her foot. "Even if I can't dance so well could I go with her?"

"Dahling," Gwenn danced away from the desk to rumple Alice's straight brown bang and to laugh into her eager brown eyes, "you can fly for them, dahling," she teased, enjoying Alice's embarrassment. "Perhaps they'll have a house for you to fly off of—smack, into an ash barrel. So you can break your arm again. Of course, dahling, you'll go with me. Won't she, Miss Jordon?"

"Well . . ."

Things were getting out of control. The smaller orphans were tired of waiting for homes and were going about their own business, with Bitsy making faces at Peter and Vance playing a game of his own on the floor. "All right," Jenifer said hastily. "The woman wants a girl of fourteen who can dance and says she'll take a younger one too. So go on."

"Oh, thank you, deah Miss Jordon."

Gwenn tripped lightly from the room, bouncing on her toes and dragging Alice who was bending over with the giggles. And Jenifer stood up.

"Here you are, Donny," she said, trying to hurry things. "It's a place in the country for a dreamy little boy. And here's one for Vance."

"I don't want to be adopted," Vance announced, wagging his head from side to side. "I'm a bear." He let out a roar to prove it and Bitsy dropped the fire tongs she was playing with.

"Vance is naughty," she shrieked, flinging short fat arms around Jenifer's knees. "He scares Bitsy."

"Pooh." Jenifer gathered the baby close to her, loving the softness of Bitsy's bright curls against her cheek. "He's only being silly. He's just a teeny-weeny baby, not half as old as you are."

"Am I older than Vance?" Bitsy leaned back to look at Jenifer and a delighted dimple flickered at the corner of her mouth. "Can I be five and go to kindergarten and let Vance be just-past-three and take a nap?"

"Sure. We'll get him a bonnet and a rattle because he's a baby."

"I'm a bear." Vance rose stiffly on what were by now his hind legs and staggered about, growling and shaking his head from side to side, and Jenifer ignored him.

"You go on, darling," she whispered to Bitsy, "and be adopted into a nice home even though Miss Jordon will miss you very much." She led Bitsy to the door, shoved her through, and after listening to the giggles that came from the hall, returned to the center of the living room.

The bear was still lurching about, his eyes shut, his head wagging, and as he circled her Jenifer reached out a long arm. "All right, Mr. Bear," she said, winking at Peter, "it's time to lock you in your cage."

Vance put up a struggle, but her hand was firmly clamped to his collar and she had him by the seat of his short blue pants. "I have a fine cage for you," she panted as Peter threw open a closet door, "and-in-you-go!"

The closet was filled with tennis rackets, old golf clubs, goloshes, and a battered saxophone of Peter's, and Vance landed in the middle of them, still roaring, but with a small boy's rage. Jenifer and Peter saluted each other, pleased with a job well done, and Jenifer was about to open the hall door to orphans who were dissatisfied with their prospective homes and were returning to the fold, when a worse commotion sounded in the yard.

"Good grief, it's the dragon!" she cried as she and Peter raced each other to the window. "She's bringing the fence and all the bushes with her."

They knelt on the window seat, rested their elbows on the sill and the children charged in to crowd around them.

Mrs. Sanders was having a tussle. She had lost control of the car, had missed the drive but not the fence and was now astride a large hibiscus bush. The motor gave an embarrassed cough, then was very still inside the hood. Mrs. Sanders' face, looking out from a bower of green, was an unbecoming shade of "shocking pink" and wisps of gray hair had jolted loose from what she called her "bun." Her heavy shoe trod on the starter and it barked back at her before the car collected itself and took off again in a leap.

"She'll never go through the garage doors," Peter prophesied, while the others cringed for Donny's bicycle, a hazard in her path.

But Mrs. Sanders managed to stop before she reached the garage or even the bicycle. She jerked on the emergency brake, gathered up her packages and ran in a skittering hop around the house.

"Something's wrong with the poor old girl," Jenifer said, backing through the children who were pressed against her. "She never acted quite that crazy before. We'd better see what it is."

She ran across the room, threw open the door of the bear's cage as she passed it, and met Mrs. Sanders in the dining room fluttering her hands and making noises like a broken record.

"I'm leaving," Mrs. Sanders cried. "I'm leaving. I'm leaving on the six o'clock train. I got a telegram and I'm leaving."

She darted back into the kitchen, excitement twitching her bony face into a landslide of wrinkles, and Jenifer, followed by her gallery, went to lean against the refrigerator.

"You mean you're really going away?" she asked, pressing her hands behind her against the cool enamel. "And leaving us, alone?"

"I have to—I got a telegram. It's somewhere here. . . ." Mrs. Sanders fumbled in her imitation leather purse and pulled out a wad of yellow paper. "It says my sister fell down and broke her hip, and I've got to go. Miss Sales, my friend at the telegraph office. . . ."

"But what about us?" Jenifer interrupted. "You promised Daddy you'd stay with us till he gets back."

"Don't no promises hold good where your blood and kin's affected." Mrs. Sanders crammed the telegram back into her purse and Jenifer said:

"I see."

"But I've got a woman comin' from the agency. She'll get here around seven and I'll come back as soon's I can. She's a real nice-lookin' person."

"I see," Jenifer said again, looking straight at Mrs. Sanders. She looked at her so long and so steadily that the woman clicked her pocketbook open and shut and wished Jenifer would turn her eyes away.

At last she did, but it was only to say to Peter, "Bring her big suitcase down from the attic and have Donny help you with her trunk."

"Law, I don't need no trunk," Mrs. Sanders laughed, relieved to be talking again. "I'm not takin' my trunk. I won't be gone more'n a few weeks."

"I said for Peter to bring your trunk."

Jenifer looked very tall standing against the refrigerator and the children stared at her, Gwenn forgetting to pose, and the others wide-eyed and fascinated. Only Peter turned away and stamped angrily up the stairs.

"Listen here, Jenifer," Mrs. Sanders found courage to say, "if you've got some highfalutin' idea that you're firin' me, you aren't. Your papa hired me, an' if there's any firin' done he'll do it."

"I'm not firing you," Jenifer answered coolly. "You said, yourself, you're leaving. When you leave you don't come back. That's all there is to it. I have Daddy's power of attorney. And now," she added pleasantly, "we'll help you pack and then you can turn the accounts over to me, and the ration points and the gas coupons. Peter will drive you to the train."

Mrs. Sanders fumbled with her purse again, uncertain whether she should go or ask to stay, but Jenifer swung herself away from the refrigerator and said to Donny, "Go on. Help Peter with the trunk."

She herded the children back to the living room, scattered them with a gesture of her hands and a warning finger against her lips; and as they melted away, on tiptoe and almost without breath, she returned to the kitchen.

Now and then in her packing Mrs. Sanders looked at the girl who was folding aprons and rolling cotton stockings into balls. There was nothing in Jenifer's face that gave a clue to her thoughts. She gathered up clothes, listened attentively to a complicated system of bookkeeping, until at last Mrs. Sanders felt compelled to ask:

"You ain't worried a bit, are you? About managin', I mean."

"Of course not." Jenifer tucked a receipted grocer's slip into the pages of the ledger without looking up. "We still have Rosie to help us and families have changed housekeepers before. There's nothing to be upset about."

But when Mrs. Sanders had gone, when Peter was back, rubbing his wheat-stubble hair and telling of the struggle he had had to get her on the train; when it was seven o'clock, then eight, then nine, and no new housekeeper had come, she sent the smaller children to bed and sat down to think the situation over.

She still had Rosie it was true, or would have when Rosie returned from her afternoon off. But Rosie was no manager. She was big-boned and willing and had trailed along with the Jordons from an army post in Kansas, but she never knew Bitsy's left rubber from the right or believed in clocks or routine. Her pale eyes looked out from under straight black hair and she was just there, with strong hands and feet that had been whipped along by

Mrs. Sanders. Now Mrs. Sanders was gone and just Rosie was there. And, Jenifer thought with a giggle, not all there at that.

Gwenn and Alice were washing dishes, and the kitchen light and their voices reached into the dusk of the back yard where she sat on a bench under a live oak tree. She stared at the garage and the vague shape of the garbage can, and when Peter slid onto the bench beside her she stopped sliding her foot back and forth in the sandy grass and said abruptly:

"Peter, let's move."

"Huh?"

"I said let's move. Over by one of the lakes."

"Jumping monkeys! There're some thirty-odd lakes in Orlando—which one and why?"

"Lake Indiola. And because we can manage better over there."

"But we haven't any house."

"I can get Mr. Cadwallader's. The one his son lived in, I mean. He'll rent it to me."

"That run-down old thing? Why, even the army officers who're stationed here in Orlando wouldn't live in it." Peter scoffed because he was bewildered, as he often was by Jenifer's mind that flew ahead of his. But when she sat without answering he put his feet up on the bench, clasped his hands around his knees and said, "Old man Cadwallader won't rent it to anybody, you know that."

"He'll rent it to me. I go over to his store nearly every day and we talk about his son. He showed me his son's things that the War Department sent home after his plane crashed and pictures of his wife and their little girl. He knows now they'll never come back to live in the house again, and one day he said it was too bad 'cause the house is made for kids. Well," Jenifer sighed then grinned, "we've got the kids."

"We sure have." Peter's hand lifted, seeking the comfort of his hair, but Jenifer reached out and stopped it.

"Just think, Peter," she said, squeezing his fingers on the bench between them, "we'd have a real garden, after we got the weeds out, and a high wall all around a big cool yard and a sandy strip of beach with a little dock and a boathouse. And the house is nice too. Oh, maybe the bathroom isn't so hot, or the kitchen, but the house isn't poky like this one. It has charm."

"And I guess we could have a canoe or something, couldn't we?"

"Sure. And Peter," Jenifer turned on the bench to lay her other hand over the two that were almost clutching each other now, "I thought we'd send for Prince Royal."

"Gosh! do you think we could?" Peter sat up and pushed her hands away. Prince Royal. His father's cavalry horse and the finest chestnut hunter a boy could ride. "Oh, Jen!" he cried, "do you suppose we could?"

"I think we'll almost have to." Jenifer was looking at Prince Royal from a practical standpoint. "We haven't much gas and you haven't a license to drive the car and I won't have time; so I think it's up to Royal to help the family some. And there's another reason I want to live over by the lake; there's a bus that goes right by the grade school."

"But what about Dad? What if he doesn't want us to move?"

"He won't care. Not when he knows I'm doing the best I can."

Jenifer's eyes looked off toward the garage again as she remembered the night she and her father had sat on the bench together. His arm had been around her and he had said, "I hate to leave you down here, honey, with so many responsibilities, and where you don't know anyone. But you can buy at the Commissary and you'll be near the army, even if you aren't in it. And you won't be cold in winter, Jenny, and if you're a little hot in summer . . . well, that will settle your clothes problem." And then he had laid his cheek against her hair and said softly, "Someday I'll make it up to you, Jenny." And they had sat quietly in the dark, loving each other and dreading tomorrow.

She and Peter sat quietly now. Jenifer had plans to make and Peter had gone a long way off on Royal. He had gone so far that he was startled to hear her say:

"I guess I won't be going back to school for the spring term."

"Won't you mind?"

"No."

"But you're supposed to graduate. You ought to graduate, Jen."

"I will, someday. I've got years and years to graduate in, but there's something else I have to do right now. I can't do it next summer or even next month. I have to do it right now, this minute. And I'd better start by going to bed so I can be up early to talk to Mr. Cadwallader. Oh,

Peter . . ." Jenifer jumped up from the bench and closed her eyes that she might see a sprawling white house and a tangled garden, "Let's pray tonight, hard, that Mr. Cadwallader will want to help us."

CHAPTER II

THE young Jordons were up early the next morning. Rosie charged back and forth across the kitchen, and Jenifer stood at the stove, expertly flipping bacon and appraising each entrant as the dining-room door swung open. "Comb your hair again," she said briefly to Alice. And to Vance: "Shoes are being worn this season." She broke eggs into hot grease, and without seeming to look at Neal who was sidling in murmured to the skillet, "The quality of mercy is not strained. It droppeth as the gentle rain from heaven in the form of the bathroom shower, first door at the head of the stairs." To Peter she said, "Hi." And she kissed the pink bow Gwenn had tied in Bitsy's curls.

Breakfast was a jolly meal. They had it in the dining room because Jenifer insisted that, with or without the dragon, a dining room was the place to eat. They talked without restraint, giggling a great deal in their new-found freedom, until Jenifer pushed back her plate and rested her arms on the table. "A new regime is starting," she announced. "We're army again."

Eight forks paused in mid-air and eight sentences were left unfinished. "It isn't going to be easy to run this family," Jenifer said. "I thought about it last night and decided on a plan. If anyone doesn't like it he can say so, but this is what I worked out." She paused a moment, waiting for their lagging minds to catch up with her, then went on. "I'll be first in command and Peter will be second. There'll be a roster for kitchen police and barracks, because we'll have to help Rosie a lot, and Peter will inspect every Saturday morning. Quarrels and failure of duty will be punished by extra k.p. and if anyone commits a really serious offense we'll hold a general court-martial. How does it sound to you?"

"Swell." Peter answered for all of them, above their shouts and suggestions, and Susan jumped up to throw her arms around Jenifer's neck and to beg:

"Can we have a flag? And put it up in the morning and take it down at night?"

"Sure we will." Peter was bursting with ideas of his own and he clapped a hand over Neal's mouth and shouted into the bedlam: "We'll have reveille and retreat. Everyone will have to get up for reveille and be home in time for retreat. If he doesn't. . . ."

"Smacko!" Alice shouted. "Spuds to peel."

"And that means really spuds," Jenifer said seriously, holding their attention and elaborating on the part of army life they preferred to forget. "Housework and homework, and maybe even sometimes washing and ironing. We'll have the flag pole and lots of fun but we'll have discipline too; and any one of you G.I. Joes who doesn't want to obey army regulations, or any command that Peter or I may give you, had better speak his piece right now."

A silence of grins answered her and she pushed back her chair and barked, "Atten*shun*. We'll work out the details tonight and we have to make a go of it; but now it's time for school. Lieutenant Jordon will take you in the staff car. Susan, your reader is in the living room; Vance, let Gwenn comb your hair. Now get off, all of you."

She helped Bitsy down from the pile of books that topped the seat of her chair, and when Peter had driven away in the car she buttoned Bitsy into her reefer and led her down the walk.

"Where're we goin', Jenifer?" Bitsy asked.

"To the grocery store to see my friend, Mr. Cadwallader."

It was dim and fragrant in the little neighborhood store. The thick rich scent of ripe bananas mingled with the heady aroma of freshly ground coffee. Fly swatters dangled from a hook; a showcase held a scattered display of lollipops and hard candy; oranges in red mesh sacks were heaped on a table, and the frozen foods refrigerator was white and shining in the gloom of potato baskets and a half-empty vegetable bin. Jenifer set Bitsy on the low refrigerator and said, "Good morning, Mr. Cadwallader," to an old man who was leaning on the candy case and looking at her over his glasses.

"Mornin'," he answered without moving. "What you want this mornin'?"

"Something awfully big." Jenifer leaned on her side of the case. She reached up and laid her arm along its cool glass top, rested her chin on her wrist and grinned across at him. "I want to rent your son's house, Mr. Cadwallader," she said.

"Holy tarnation! Why you . . . you . . . you young upstart!" Mr. Cadwallader began to sputter like a long string of firecrackers and Jenifer let him go until he reached one last pop on the end. Then, her chin still resting on her arm, her eyes on his, she said:

"Don't say anything more until I explain a few things to you. You see, it's like this. . . ."

Half an hour later Mr. Cadwallader sat in his small cluttered office at the back of his store, Bitsy on his lap. What gray hair he had was standing up in a fringe and he was looking ruefully at Jenifer on a splint-bottom chair beside him.

"Danged if I can see how you're goin' to manage," he muttered, "but I reckon you can. If you've got to take care of all those kids, an' it seems as if you do, then Jim's house is the place for you to do it in. But don't you let 'em go and drown in the lake."

"I won't," Jenifer promised.

"And don't you let 'em fall out of the rowboat if I decide to unfasten the padlock." He leaned across Bitsy who was busy with a rubber stamp and took some keys from a drawer. "This one's to the stable," he said frowning at it. "What about that rig you're wantin'? Think your horse can pull a rig?"

"Well, if he can't he can learn." Jenifer leaned forward eagerly. "Any horse ought to be willing to pull a carriage in wartime, don't you think?"

" 'Twould seem so." Mr. Cadwallader went on looking at the keys and frowning until at last he burst out, "Dang it, I'm worried. It ain't right for you to be so young an' . . ."

"But I'm getting older every day. I'm twenty-four hours older right this minute than I was the last time you saw me. I'm hurrying as fast as I can." Jenifer laughed but Mr. Cadwallader only shook his head.

"Maybe I'd better send Lacey over to stay with you," he said uncertainly. "Lacey ain't so old either, or so sensible, but she's five years older'n you are."

"Lacey's wonderful." Jenifer reached over and laid her hand on his shirt sleeve. "She's the most beautiful girl I ever saw and you know you're so proud of her you almost burst. Why, you're always saying, 'dang it, my girl Lacey she's smart; she's smarter'n I am. Teachin' in the high school . . .'" Jenifer mimicked him and they both laughed but she added seriously, "Lacey has all she can do, Mr. Cadwallader, but if it worries you she can look us over sometimes and I'll come to you for advice. Oh, dear, darling Mr. Cadwallader," she cried, jumping up and throwing her arms around his thin shoulders almost unseating Bitsy, "you're the most wonderful man! And we'll keep your beautiful house simply shining!"

"And we *must*," she told the children a few days later when they were tying clothes into sheets and piling up comforts and blankets. "Not many people would be so good to us."

They had declared a holiday from school in order to move and Jenifer was sitting on a mattress balancing her checkbook. "Golly, it's costing a lot," she said to Peter who, squatting on one end of the mattress, was scraping the broken end of a lamp cord. "I do hope we can make three truckloads do it. Did you buy all the things we need?"

"Yeah." Peter inspected the exposed copper wire, twisted it and fitted it into the socket while he talked. "And I got a good flagpole out at the lumber yard; they're going to make it for me. And I went out to the Army Base to see if I could find a sergeant I know. I thought he might help me put it up."

"Will he?"

"I didn't see him. But a lieutenant was wandering about, a snappy-looking dude, and he brought me home. We drove by the house to have a look around, the new place I mean, and he thought we should fasten the pole to the boat house. He said it would be a cinch to do that."

"Oh, Peter, the flag would look pretty flying out over the lake, wouldn't it?"

"Andy's going to help me fix it some Sunday."

"Andy?"

"The lieutenant. He said just to call him Andy."

"What's he like?"

"Who?"

"The lieutenant, stupid." Jenifer laid her checkbook in her lap and asked dreamily, "Is he fine of form and fair of face?"

"He's a big rugged guy. And he has a scar on his forehead that he got in a raid over Germany, and he's gimpy."

"Gimpy?"

"He limps."

"What's he doing here, out at the Air Force School, if he's been in combat?"

"I don't know; teaching while he rests up, I guess."

The cord was finished now and Peter crawled over to

an outlet to test it. Jenifer, alone on a raft in a sea of activity, went on struggling with figures until the truck came. Then furniture bumped down the stairs, and an army couple who were taking over the house arrived and got in the way while they poked about, measuring and planning and crowding the Jordons out.

"Bitsy, Vance, get in the car and stay there," Jenifer ordered, standing in the hall and retying the red ribbon that held back her hair. "Neal, you and Susan can carry out the small things." She wore a blue and white striped jersey tucked into navy blue shorts, her favorite uniform for housework, and with her hands on her hips inspected every load that passed her. "Stop that victrola," she called upward. "This isn't a gala performance, Gwenn. Walk! Flat on your feet."

The new renters pushed into the hall with her, and having had but a few months' acquaintance with the army watched her generalship in open-mouthed amazement. "We're used to it," she said, guiding Donny, blind behind a carton of kitchen utensils. "You should see us when the furniture comes and goes in crates. Alice, put Mother's silver coffee service on the back seat of the car."

Alice staggered by with a silver tray that held a collection of urns and teapots and cream and sugars, and the new renters shuddered at such valuable family heirlooms making their way across the grass with nothing between them and the ground but a small girl's stomach. Alice was bent into a cakewalk but Jenifer turned carelessly away without waiting to see if she reached the car.

"I think I'll go now," she said, as the driver fastened the

tailboard on his truck, "so I'll be on the receiving end. Peter will take over here. Good-by."

She flashed down the steps, swung herself into the cab of the truck, and flanked by moving men bounced happily toward her new home.

The house was even lovelier in the morning sunlight than she had dreamed, because now it was hers. White and low, it crouched under live oaks cool and blinking lazily at her. Its side porch was asleep, leaning tiredly against the dining room; the kitchen floor sagged in well-earned weariness; and the dark center hall that cut through the house in a T cracked crossly at her. But the living room wakened with the opening of its shutters and became gay again, its walls abloom with roses growing out of a pale green carpet that had faded a little since a young soldier had gone away. Sunbeams danced in through small-paned windows, exploring corners, the white mantel, and the empty bookshelves.

"Dear darling house," Jenifer cried, running along the dark hall to throw open bedroom doors for the movers. "I do adore you so!"

"Girls' barracks to the right," she called from the front door when Peter arrived with the car piled high with odds and ends and children. "Boys' to the left. Peter, your quarters are at the end and I'm next to you with Bitsy, and Rosie has a room off the kitchen. Double time, everybody, so we can have a look around before dark."

She flew about, unpacking sheets, seeing that each army trunk locker stood at the foot of its owner's bed in true soldier fashion, allotting closet space and dresser drawers; then, hugging herself because no one else was near enough to hug, she stood in the garden and showed them their estate.

"It's all ours!" she cried, looking around and gloating. "The shrubbery, the weeds, and the cement wall; the jaquaranda tree and the palms and the flowers; and even the pebbles in the path and the stable with its curlycues on the roof. And the lake's ours, too, just as much of it as we want to row on or swim in or dip out. We can sit on the bench on top of our very own boat house and. . . ."

"And run our flag up and down!" Alice was squinting into the sky, secretly scheming, wrapping her legs around an imaginary pole, going up, hand over hand. . . . But Peter brought her down with a crash.

"You're no flagpole sitter," he growled, "so don't you let me catch you trying it. And no flying off the stable either; that belongs to the car and to Royal. Golly, Royal's going to love it here."

"And he'll love the nice green grass. He's going to mow the grass with his big strong teeth," Jenifer chanted, running about the lawn and planning where Bitsy's swing would hang. "Hi there, Mr. Cadwallader!"

Mr. Cadwallader was trotting around the side of the house, an unusual gait for him, and mopping his bald head as he came. "Dang it, if you kids don't beat the record for speed," he complained, shaking his large red handkerchief and mopping again. "Lacey said I'd best get here and stop you from cookin'. I can't see any sense to it but she's bringing a picnic basket with her."

"She *is?* Oh, Mr. Cadwallader! That's *wonderful!*" Jenifer dragged forward a canvas chair and leaned over to help him into its sagging depth.

"Don't be so fussy over me," he grunted petulantly. "I kin sit down by myself, been doing it over a good many years. Git away, Jenifer," he said, giving her a push and letting himself down carefully. "Lacey'd abeen here sooner if she hadn't stopped to pick up one of your boys."

"One of our . . ." Jenifer looked at the children, some by the lake and some by the stable, and then she exclaimed, "Neal isn't here! I hadn't missed him."

"Well, he's here now." Mr. Cadwallader pointed behind her where a round-cropped head was peeking around the side of the house. Like a labored drawing the head slowly acquired a body in overalls and a hand that held a rope. On the other end of the rope was a dog.

"I reckon he's made another adoption," Mr. Cadwallader remarked laconically while Jenifer stared. "I reckon nine mouths to feed ain't enough for him. You'd best go over there," he said, reaching in his pocket for his pipe, "since it seems he ain't acomin' over here."

Jenifer walked across the lawn and looked down at Neal and the strange canine structure that stood beside him. It was a dog, no doubt about it, although it looked more like a mop that had been swiped across a dirty floor. It was small and woolly, gray and white in patches, and nature, for a joke, had given it a frowsy, lovable Teddy Bear face.

"This is Rollo," Neal explained, his own round face looking up with the same pleading expression Rollo wore. "The dogcatcher man was after him."

"How do you do, Rollo." Jenifer knelt down and the little dog promptly hung out a red plush flag and whipped erect a feather duster.

"Miss Lacey thinks he's pretty," Neal said, full of pride, while Rollo adored Jenifer with both ends of him. "Do you like him?"

"Well," Jenifer wiped the puppy's greeting from her face and stood up, "having just met him," she said, "I hardly know him." She looked down at Rollo who had seated himself, his head on one side, with the expectant smile of an invited guest, and added, "But you might take him down to the lake and introduce him to the others. And Neal," she leaned over to whisper, "don't tell Rollo I said so—but I think he's kind of cute." Then she saw Lacey's gray coupe in the drive and ran toward it.

Lacey Cadwallader was, as Jenifer had told Mr. Cadwallader, a beautiful girl. She had black hair that curled around her face in a very un-schoolmarmish fashion, and she was so richly bronzed from Florida sunshine that her teeth flashed very white and even and her eyes seemed electrically blue.

"Jenifer, you bad girl," she said, handing out a basket, "aren't you coming back to school?"

"I don't see how I can, Miss Lacey; not for a while at any rate."

"But, darling, you're almost ready to graduate."

"Yes, I know." Jenifer stood holding the basket. She held it lightly, untired and strong. "I'm having a lovely time," she said. "It's adventure." She looked toward the lake and quoted softly:

"To savor each day's fare, the salt, the sugar,
Not to taste, but to enjoy the flavor;
To live each hour, and not to measure
Sparingly. . . ."

She broke off and began walking across the grass, and
Lacey catching up with her asked:

"What was that you quoted, Jenifer?"

"I don't know; just something that popped into my
head, I guess."

"It was something you wrote yourself, wasn't it?"

"Maybe." Jenifer spoke carelessly and swung her basket, smiling a little, and Lacey wished she could see behind that mischievous, secret look.

"It's such a pity, darling," she began, "when you have
so much talent . . . I wish. . . ."

"Don't." Jenifer set down the basket and stood quite
still. She was serious now and her eyes were deep and
gray and as unfathomable as the ocean. "I'm happy, Miss
Lacey, really," she said softly. "I love every minute of
every day, and . . . Why, I think I'm the happiest person
in the whole world. And Peter's happy too." She looked at
the children playing with the new puppy and ended,
"Don't worry about us. Don't waste one single minute
worrying."

CHAPTER III

THE sun was taking his time about rising and beginning what Jenifer called "Prince Royal's Day," and the Jordons had beaten him up by an hour. Beds were made, dishes washed, and by the time the sun had got his furnaces stoked and burning brightly the Jordons were shivering beside a box car, watching Prince Royal come daintily down a ramp.

Peter led him, talking softly to him, and Royal came in a minuet. He placed each foot carefully, and with a worried eye on his audience executed a leap at the end that scattered Jordons in all directions.

"Whoa there, old man, steady," Peter said, patting his bronze neck to quiet him. But Royal wasn't interested in a family reunion. His fancy was caught by some tufts of grass. He felt fine to be out of the box car with his legs working properly, not eternally scrambling for a foothold, and he pranced a bit and threw his head about.

Peter let him play until the carload of Jordons had gone to prepare another reception, before he and Royal started home, linked in happy communion by Royal's halter rope.

It was pleasant strolling along the streets, quiet in the early morning, and Peter whistled or sometimes grinned just for the pure joy of living. He had a horse; a handsome high-stepping horse that left nothing more to be desired of life. Royal, on the other hand, was stepping out because he had a boy. His memory, small, and lost somewhere between his cocked ears and the white blaze on his forehead, was returning. Once, long ago, he had nipped at

Peter's shoulder, so now he nipped at it again, playfully, and with no curiosity about where he was going or what would happen to him next.

But when he was led into the stable, between the car and a strange thing with shafts, he expressed his disapproval. Another stall confronted him and he was tired of stalls. The whole family, since it was Saturday, was patient with him. The children ran about showing him his deep straw bed, his hay that was stacked along the wall in bales, and tried to make him look into the tack room where hung his saddle and bridle and his fine black driving harness.

The children gave their whole day to Royal; sitting on the grass while Peter grazed him; sitting on stools and buckets while Peter groomed him; and when Peter mounted him and went riding off around the lake they simply sat. In time, they knew, Royal would come home to have his supper and then Peter would let them hand him things.

For several days Royal trotted off to seek adventure and with only Peter to share it. Donny was given a turn around the block and Alice and Gwenn a quiet walk around the yard, that left all three unsatisfied. Another gas coupon went for work Royal was supposed to do, and Jenifer decided to take a hand.

The idea struck her in the middle of the afternoon when the children were at school and Bitsy was on the side porch with her dolls and Rollo. An idea to Jenifer was an order from the High Command. So she rushed off to don her jodhpurs, stopping only to look in the girls' barracks

at a bathrobe and slippers on the floor, and to write on a
blackboard that had replaced a mirror in the hall, "Extra
k.p. for Gwenn. Mopping kitchen, Thursday, 4 P.M." Then
she marched out to the stable where Royal was taking a
nap.

"My friend," she announced, leaning on the stall door
and pulling his tail to wake him, "you've had a nice vacation and now it's time to go to work."

Royal shifted to his other two legs and watched through
half-closed eyes while Jenifer rolled the carriage out onto
the graveled driveway and brought his harness from the
tack room. He was docile about coming out of his stall
and was even interested in all the things she was hanging
on him. He accepted the buckled neck strap and breast-
band, and only grunted when she tightened the girth of
the narrow saddle pad with its nickel rings and studded
trimmings; but he resented the things she tried to slip
around his rear. It was touch and go in the stable door,
with Jenifer circling warily and Royal straining against a
chain fastened in the wall, white of eye, his ears laid back,
and his dancing shoes striking sparks on the brick floor.

But Jenifer won. She was hot and tired when she got
him dressed and Royal's head was drooping, both from
shame and the weight of leather lines that were rolled and
dangling like misplaced earrings from his bit. He followed
her meekly from the barn and stood lost in his own troubled thoughts, refusing to admire the carriage with her.

It was a handsome equipage, or had been in its day;
and even now it had a haughty look, as if it snubbed the
streamlined monster that had crowded it off the road. It

held its fringed top with elegance, proud that its two high seats were hard and narrow, made for Victorian ladies who never lounged. It had the genteel, and faintly musty odor of the past, as if standing alone on its yellow wheels it had clung to the dreams and secrets of men and women long since gone.

Jenifer knew what the carriage had seen; and when the children were helping Peter cover its scars with black enamel, she had lifted imaginary flounces to set her foot daintily on the high step. With a flurry of lace and ruffles, she settled herself on the seat and was as coquettishly gay as a Southern belle. Or, scrambling up in front, she propped her shoes on the cracked leather dash, hunched over to hold imaginary lines between her knees, and was a farmer looking out across his land, proud, and pointing to his citrus groves and his cattle.

Now she tried to instill a certain amount of romantic interest into Royal who would have none of it. When she walked him along the drive, pretending they were going for a stroll, he followed pleasantly; but when she tried a quick reversal that would swing him under the lifted shafts he was cleverer than she was.

She led him endlessly. She tried to pull him to the carriage, tried to pull the carriage up to him; and the only time he surprised them both by walking straight between the yellow poles, he and the carriage faced each other and she had to back him out.

"Listen, you," she panted, trying to push him sideways, "get over there."

But half a ton of Royal was more than she could manage. So she mopped her face and tied him to a palm tree.

"Dang it," she muttered in Mr. Cadwallader's best language, sitting down to deliver him a lecture, "you're the stubbornest horse that ever lived. Think of all the money I spent to get you here. And what are you doing for me? Not a thing! Are you helping anybody? Are you helping win the war?" Royal turned his head away and Jenifer answered for him, "You certainly aren't. And I've a good notion to send you right back to the remount depot, where you came from. It would serve you right if you had to go back to living in a pasture again, with a lot of other horses that bite and kick."

An army jeep stopped at the gate and she twisted around to look at it. "Even that little thing does better than you do," she jeered at Royal.

An officer was climbing out of the jeep and Jenifer watched him come along the drive. He was young and well-built, and his overseas cap rode on waves of sunburnt hair, cockily, like the paper ships Neal made; and he had a humorous face, in spite of thatched roofs for eyebrows and a lower lip that protruded in a pout even when it was extended in a wide and crooked grin.

"Hi," he said, smiling with gay tan eyes at Jenifer. "I'm Andy Compton."

"Oh, hello." Jenifer scrambled to her feet and wiped her hand on her jodhpurs before she held it out. "I'm Peter's sister, Jenifer," she said. "He's told me of you and we've been hoping you'd come to see us. Shall we go and sit in the garden?"

"I can't stay. I drove my boss in town on business and

thought I'd look you up while I wait for him. How's Peter?"

"Fine. He's still at school."

They looked at each other with the casual interest people always feel at a first meeting; Jenifer liking his crooked lower lip, and he the easy way she stood, her hands clasped loosely together. Then he looked at Royal who was boredly staring at nothing and asked politely:

"Were you just going for a drive?"

"I was trying to." Jenifer began to laugh and they were friends. "You see, we've never driven Royal," she explained, "and it looks as if we never will. I can't even get him into the carriage shafts."

"Want some help?"

"I'd love it."

The way they set to work boded no good for Royal. The young lieutenant took off his blouse and dropped it on the grass as if he'd been looking a long time for a fight, and when he flung his cap beside it Jenifer saw that his hair was golden-red, not sunburned. Looking at his stubborn lower lip that had a jaw to match it, Jenifer untied Royal from the palm tree and thought it would be fun to watch two redheads battle each other.

Andy seemed to have forgotten he had pressing duties with the army. He backed Royal in line with the carriage and fixing upon him an eye that meant no nonsense, clamped his hands like bear traps to the bit and motioned Jenifer to lower the shafts. She eased them down and Royal, ignorant of what went on behind, was unaware that he had lost his freedom. But the harness was a dif-

ferent matter. Neither Jenifer nor Andy knew where or
what all the straps and buckles should fasten.

"I'll tell you what we'd better do," Andy said from his
post at the head, after Royal was coupled to the carriage
and they still had some odds and ends left over, "I'll just
walk along and lead him so he gets the hang of the thing.
We'll figure out the harness later."

"All right, let's go."

Jenifer moved away from the carriage and Andy took a
firm step backward. Royal, perforce, went too. He moved
two unwilling feet and something shoved him from behind. That was enough for Royal. He rose straight up in
the air. He pawed, he twisted. Andy clung to the bit and
Royal struck out around him. The carriage scattered
gravel, something snapped and it teetered wildly, its fine
fringe waving.

"Hang onto him!" Jenifer screamed. "One of the traces
broke."

"I've got him," Andy grunted in answer and wondered
if he had. "Whoa, Royal, whoa!" he yelled, being jerked
along like a puppet. "Take it easy."

But Royal had no thought of taking it at all. He pawed
and lunged, terrified of the thing that was fastened to
him, and hoping to get free. Bitsy's screams and Rollo's
shrill barking from the porch added to the bedlam and
Jenifer, trying to keep the carriage upright, saw they were
nearing the gate.

"If only I dared unhook the other trace," she moaned,
fearing that Royal, once he found he was free, would bolt
and Andy couldn't hold him. They were bearing down on

the jeep that was parked outside and she knew that even if Royal managed to miss it the carriage couldn't. Then she saw Peter coming. Peter, with Susan and Neal and Vance.

After it was over they told her she had screamed.

She couldn't remember but she thought she might have, for Peter looked up and saw them. He gave the children a shove toward safety and ran for the iron gates. It looked as if he couldn't make them, but he did. He clanged them shut and whirled, flattened against them and with his arms outstretched, just in time to stop Royal in a desperate plunge.

"There, baby, there," he crooned, stroking the horse's sweating neck. "It's all right now."

Royal's head nuzzled against him and when Andy loosed his hold on the bit he stood on trembling legs, his wet sides heaving, while Peter went on talking softly to him. "It's all right, boy," Peter said, stroking and talking. And then he said to Andy without a change in his tone, "Was your leg hurt any? Gee, that's good. Do you think you could help Jen cut him loose?"

When the carriage was back in the stable and Royal was wearing his halter again Peter let him graze. Andy had worked the numbness from his hands and Jenifer was helping him into his blouse.

"I'm terribly sorry we let you in for such a bad time," she said, brushing grass from his cap before she gave it to him. "I hope you won't be afraid to come and see us again."

"I'll be back." Andy looked at Royal who was nibbling contentedly near Peter's feet. "I'm going for a drive behind that horse of yours if it's the last thing I ever do. I'd do it now if I didn't have to get back with the jeep. He hasn't licked me . . . yet."

Jenifer looked at Andy's stubborn face and laughed. And Peter called across the yard: "We'll try it again on Sunday if you're game."

"I'm game. But we'll put up the flag pole first while I'm still in one piece and able to do it. I'll be seeing you on Sunday."

They watched him climb into his jeep and chug away, and then as Jenifer started toward the house, Peter said:

"You shouldn't have done it, Jen."

"Done what? Let Andy help me?"

"No, tried to make Royal pull the carriage."

"Well, for goodness' sake." Jenifer stopped and looked at Peter. "Have you lost your mind?" she asked. "That's what we brought him here for, wasn't it?"

"Yes, I guess so, but. . . ." Peter looked down at the rope in his hands, fumbling for words. "Royal just isn't the working type," he said slowly.

"Nor am I." Jenifer laughed then came back to say gently, "Peter, do you see that house? It has beds to make, dishes to wash, and cooking to be done. We all have jobs. And Royal has a job. He's lucky there isn't any cavalry in this war. His job's a pipe compared to what he might have got."

"Yes, I know."

"Then don't coddle him."

"Okay." Peter looked at Royal who was so happy now. "I know you're right, Jen," he sighed, "but, gosh, I wish I could pull the darn thing for him."

CHAPTER IV

JENIFER lay in bed and waited. It was Sunday, and she snuggled down under the covers wishing Peter would forget to blow his saxophone. He never did. On school days she was glad to hear him tooting reveille right on the dot and with only a few false notes; but when Saturday and Sunday came she wished he and his alarm clock would oversleep. The clock was as faithful as Peter. At six-thirty it clapped its little hands together and raised its happy voice. Then Peter grabbed the saxophone, and standing in the middle of the back yard he blew in the dawn. Rollo joined in too with a neighbor's chickens, and by the time the Jordons had poured out of the house in answer to the summons Peter had pitched Royal his breakfast food of hay.

Jenifer was always the last to arrive, due to lacing Bitsy's shoes, and it was her job to look at the line in its odd assortment of garments, and to yawn, "all present and accounted for." After today they would raise the flag.

At the thought of the flag she sat up in bed with a jerk. Andy was coming to dinner, and so was Lacey, and she had to help Rosie roast a leg of lamb and bake some pies. She threw back the covers as Peter went charging along the hall, and was wide awake and a little excited that a thrilling new day had begun.

Children ran to and fro. The table was set for the midday meal in its best lace mats and a flat dish of floating red blossoms, before they left for Sunday school. The porch was swept, the lawn chairs dusted, and by twelve o'clock the small-sized Jordons were swinging on the gates, watching the road. The gates wore a homemade sign that said "beware of the dog" and Rollo was doing his loudest to live up to it.

Andy was the first to arrive, walking from the bus at the corner, and he stood in the yard with Jenifer and Peter and looked dubiously at the crowd that surrounded him.

"It's no use repeating their names again," Jenifer said, positive and frank about it. "You couldn't remember. You'll just have to keep working on it yourself."

He was doing his best when Lacey drove in. "Now let me see," he was saying, "you're Susan, with the pigtails. And you, the dark one, you're Gwenn. No, Alice? Yeah, that's right, Alice. And the boy over there on the bench. . . ." And then he saw Lacey coming toward him.

"Wow!" he said, his eyes shining like freshly polished leather. "Is that another one? If so . . ."

"That's Lacey Cadwallader." Jenifer, who was ready with formal introductions, understood why Andy was staring so.

Lacey wore a pale pink suit over a white sweater. Her black hair was parted in the middle and drawn tightly back into a chignon that fanned out in a gleaming roll on her coat collar and she looked as smart as though she had stepped from a page in a fashion magazine.

Andy was holding her hand and grinning down at her, crookedly and with pleasure. Then he sighed and shook his head. "Dear, dear," he said, "what a pity."

"A pity?" Up jerked Lacey's eyebrows and she took her hand away.

"A pity you aren't a Jordon," he explained. "I've just been hired as coachman and general handy man. I'd like the job lots better if I knew you'd be around to give me orders."

"But Lacey *is* around," Gwenn exclaimed. "She . . ."

"*Aunt* Lacey, Gwenn," Jenifer said sternly. "I've told you children you must always say Aunt Lacey."

"And Uncle Andy. Don't forget I'm your uncle, too." Andy winked at Gwenn and grinned at the back of Lacey's head that had turned away. "We're your old aunt and uncle come to spend the day," he said. "Now entertain us."

Jenifer entertained them by letting them sit on kitchen stools and watch her put finishing touches to the dinner. But Andy couldn't stay on his stool.

"Boy, what pies," he sniffed, crouching with her beside the oven. "I'll bet Aunt Lacey never made custard pies like these."

"I make delicious pies," Lacey said complacently, reaching into the cupboard behind her for a dish Alice wanted. "All my . . . *friends* . . . adore my pies."

"Think of that!" He got up and followed Jenifer to the sink. "Isn't it sad," he asked, leaning on one elbow and nibbling a radish, "to have to count your friends by your cooking?"

"It's better than not to count them at all." Lacey tossed her head and Andy shook his finger at her.

"Now, now, Aunt Lacey," he admonished, "watch your temper. I'm the one who has red hair."

Jenifer looked from one to the other and laughed. It

was quite evident they had not got off to a placid friendship; and while she was disappointed she hoped with time
and opportunity they might do better. If the government
could provide the time, she decided, she was more than
willing to provide the opportunity.

Andy was a dynamo of energy. When dinner was over
and Rosie looked eager for an afternoon off, he led Gwenn
to the sink, handed Alice a tea towel, whipped an apron
onto Lacey and gave Jenifer a push through the back
door.

"Shoo," he said. "Go off and rest someplace. You've done
more than your share, so go out and play with Peter."

When Jenifer found the door was locked against her
pleading she philosophically followed the path that led to
the lake. Beyond the garden a point of land dropped off
abruptly and under it a small boat house rested its back
against the cliff. Its flat roof was level with the lawn and
she walked out on it to lean over the rail and look at water
lapping against the supporting piles and flowing into open
doors below her. Peter whistled to her and she turned to
watch him walk carefully down a slope in the lawn that
led to the lake, carrying a twelve foot pole and a box of
tools.

"Hey," he said, standing below her on a dock that was
merely a platform with two wide planks extended beyond
it over the water. "Hoist the flagpole up there while I go
back for the braces."

Jenifer reached over the rail and grasped a smooth
round knob. She slid her hands under a small pulley with

dangling ropes, and lifted. As the pole went up Peter raised his arms to steady it and when it swung out and away from him he shouted, "Ow!" Jenifer dropped the flagpole on the boathouse deck and looked over the rail again. There was no Peter. No splash, no ripples; nothing.

"Peter?" she called in a small voice, leaning far out and trying to see under the planking. "Peter?"

"Huh?" His head peeked around from inside the boat-house door and he said, "Gee, you almost knocked me out."

He was on his knees, clinging to a narrow catwalk, a broken relic of the days when people had time and gasoline for speed boats, and he got carefully to his feet, saying ruefully as he rubbed his head, "I thought I was a goner and still don't see how I managed to land in here."

Jenifer laughed at him and then forgot him. She sat down on a wooden bench that advertised in large red letters: A. CADWALLADER—STAPLE AND FANCY GROCERIES. She had some problems to solve, such as where could she buy more milk should Lacey and Andy stay for a pick-up supper, and would the lamb go around again. Her thoughts were inclined to wander off unless she kept them tethered and she was glad when she saw the dishwashers racing down the path.

She and Lacey shared the bench while the boys put up the pole. It was a lazy afternoon, warm in the sunshine, and even Royal was in a pleasant mood. He took six halting steps with the carriage.

"I think he ought to come to the ceremonies," Jenifer

said, pleased with Royal but disappointed because Peter wouldn't let him try again. "You could ride him, Peter, and wear Daddy's saber."

So at five o'clock it was a strange assemblage that stood retreat on the Jordon lawn. Donny was posted on the boathouse deck and stood staring up at the flag, proudly rearing back against the ropes he held, waiting for his signal. His color guard, comprised of Neal and Susan, was ready, if the pulley worked, to gather the descending folds into lifted arms. Royal, in the foreground, watched everything with interest while Peter sat stiffly in the saddle and practised drawing his saber from its scabbard. The leftovers were lined up behind him, with Rollo on a leash, and they waited in nervous fervor. Their task was to sing the National Anthem, since Peter couldn't hope to play it on the saxophone, and they cleared their throats and wondered how they would know when to start out together.

At last Peter's saber flashed upward and held rigid at his chin. "Oh say, can you see," they sang, "by the dawn's early light." Lacey's soprano and Andy's rich baritone led them and Vance threw back his little head and sang as if the superintendent of schools were watching him. A breeze caught the flag, stretching the red and white stripes and the stars against a flaming sunset, and from under their saluting hands the singers watched it slide slowly down to Neal and Susan. Then Peter trotted away on Royal and the others walked back to the house.

"You're a funny family," Andy said that evening, lying on the living room floor before the fire and listening to

Jenifer send Vance and Bitsy to bed. "Do the kids always mind like this?"

"Most always." Jenifer looked up from whispering to Bitsy. "Who's turn is it to see them in tonight?" she asked.

"It's mine," Susan sighed. "At least that's what Gwenn said is written on the blackboard."

"All right, then get 'em in. And who takes you and Neal?"

"Alice. Gwenn said that, too."

"Then I guess she does, if Gwenn can read. Well, run along, you've only fifteen minutes."

Andy watched the children leave the room. "You ought to see my sister's kids," he muttered, lying back and crossing his arms under his head. "The little brats take all the conversation at mealtime and then whine and yell when they have to go to bed so we can have what's left of the evening."

"Why doesn't your sister punish them?"

"Ye gods, she does. And every time I'm out there their father has to whale 'em."

Jenifer laughed and slid back over the carpet to rest her head against Lacey's knees and to grin up at her. "They should use our method, shouldn't they, Lacey?" she said. "One good court martial ought to fix them."

"How do you hold a court martial?" Andy asked the question idly, amused and mildly curious, but Alice who was lying on her stomach and sorting stamps with Donny looked around and said:

"I'm being tried tomorrow night."

"Huh?" Andy sat up and stared. "What for?"

"Well, you see, I stole Donny's bicycle. He said I couldn't have it so I took it anyway. We had a fight about it." She studied a stamp she held before passing it over to Donny, and he, after a grunted thanks, explained:

"I couldn't let her use it 'cause I had to pass my papers."

"But Jenifer wanted some stuff from the store. . . ."

"Be careful, Alice." Neal, who had been but a sleepy ball in an oversized chair, managed to prop his eyes open long enough to say, "You might pred . . . pred-u-ju-dice the members of the court."

"What's *he* got to do with it?" Andy asked.

"Neal? Why, he's my defense counsel."

"Oh, ye gods!" Andy fell back on the floor again but Alice said complacently:

"He's pretty good."

Andy looked at Neal with new respect. Up to now he had been just another little boy who made his share of dishes to be washed, who had a name to be remembered, and nothing much about him to make one want to use his name. But as a capable lawyer who hadn't even learned to read yet . . . Andy grinned and asked, "Could I look in on a court sometime?"

"No." Jenifer shook her head and answered for them all. "But you and Lacey could sit on a court," she added, "if you'd like to. We need some good unbiased minds."

"I can't come tomorrow night but have you another case scheduled after Alice?"

"I'll go see." Jenifer got up and went into the hall to consult the bulletin board. When she came back she stood in the door and looked sheepishly at Andy. "Yes, we have," she said. "It's me."

"Oh gosh, not *you*. Don't tell me the commanding officer gets tried!"

"Umhum," Jenifer nodded. "We do it that way. You see, I spanked Vance and Peter said . . ."

"Don't tell me." Andy scrambled to his feet and waved his hands to stop her. "As a member of the court it's better for me not to know." Then he grinned and turned to Lacey. "Come on, Aunt Lacey," he said, "let's go home before they try us, too, for wearing out our welcome."

CHAPTER V

IT WAS a still and peaceful day. Jenifer sat on the boathouse deck, her back against A. CADWALLADER—STAPLE AND FANCY GROCERIES, her feet propped against the rail. Her eyes were closed and she was listening to the quiet. No shrill screams of children set the sound waves rocking and no yapping of Rollo threw them into a tempest. The children were gone for the afternoon. They were strung from Mr. Cadwallader's store through the Scouts to a high school play, and Jenifer was alone at her end of the line.

She watched a breeze trying to blow water scollops into waves, listened to a slap-slap against the boathouse piles that meant little runs for freedom had ended in nothing but more water, and read a bit and dreamed a bit and then, with a mighty yawn and a sigh, discovered she was bored.

To be bored, for Jenifer, was something novel. She might be tired, exhausted into frazzled apathy, but her mind always urged her body on like a giant with a stick. Now her mind slept. It became hypnotized by the pattern of the waves while her body wanted to go. Just where Jenifer didn't know but she got up from the bench, yawned her way around the house, and struck off down the lane.

At the corner she paused. There were sidewalks here and prim lawns with carefully-tended shrubbery. There was also another lake. It was a small well-groomed lake, flowing neatly to its grassy banks; the kind of lake which

61

provided a setting for two majestic swans and houses that were built to face it.

Jenifer, for lack of something better to do, sat sidewise on another bench, a carved stone structure set in a landscaped plot, and stared at a house beyond the guarding street. It was a white and shining mansion, large enough for a hotel or a country club, and she rested her arms and her chin on the back of the bench, wondering how it would feel to live in such a place.

The house had no need for a wall around it for no peddler would set foot on the spotless circular drive, and Jenifer thought even a car would hang onto all its cylinders lest they drip so much as a drop of oil. She even wondered if the people who owned it weren't afraid to leave their fingerprints on the great white door.

She was lost in imagining herself as mistress of the house when a voice behind her said:

"Would you mind frightfully turning your head a little? I'd like to catch your profile."

Jenifer turned her head, but she swung her whole body around with it in order to look at a boy who was sitting under a tree with a sketchbook on his lap.

"Now you've ruined it," he said, frowning at her. "You were nice just the way you were and it was stupid of me to ask you to move."

He was an odd-looking boy. His face was very thin and he had dark long-lashed eyes that seemed to have burned all the color out of his white skin. Only his mouth looked alive, as if it and his eyes, together, had battled the life from the rest of his face. His brown hair was wavy and worn too long, in the careless effect movie actors have stolen from artists and poets; and studying him, Jenifer thought that but for his modern white cardigan and carefully creased gray slacks he might have posed for Percy Bysshe Shelley sitting with a pencil clasped between sensitive nervous fingers.

"Oh. Were you drawing me?" she asked, so dissatisfied with the lack of brilliance in her answer that when he said, "I was trying to if you'd just hold still a moment," she obediently rested her chin on her arms again and let herself dwell on his accent.

That he was a winter guest she knew. No one could live in Florida and be so pale. His speech was clipped and his A so broad she was about to settle him in Boston when suddenly he said, "There you are," and she was rocked with the thought that he might be British.

She got up from the bench and walked over to look down at the drawing.

"Why, it's good!" she exclaimed, seeing herself in her baggy sweater, with her knees crossed and a faraway dreamy look in her pose. "It's really good."

"Not much. You may have it if you like."

He held the sketch up to her but Jenifer shook her head. "Thank you, but I couldn't take it," she said. "You'd better keep it; it might be valuable some day."

"No chance of that." He dropped the sketch carelessly on the grass and was straightening pages of his portfolio, preparing to close it, when Jenifer sat down beside him.

"May I see some of your drawings?" she asked.

Without a word he passed the book to her and looked

indifferently at the lake while she turned the pages. "Oh, I love this one," she said chattily, "the one of the old man. It's even better than the picture of me. And this one— part of a garden and a door." She looked up but he was scowling at the swans that were floating by like two ala- baster decorations. "This is a pear vine that grows on a wall like our grapes, isn't it?" she asked. "I'd love to see one."

"It's a bit of our garden at home."

"In England?"

"Yes."

"Tell me about it." Jenifer laid the book in her lap and clasped her fingers over its edge. "You're lonely, aren't you?"

"Not lonely, no." He leaned back against the tree trunk and Jenifer prodded:

"Homesick?"

"I can't say that. It's just that a chap . . ." He broke off and reached for his sketchbook, but she held it tightly.

"Please," she said, "I haven't finished looking." She turned another page then asked abruptly, "How long have you been over here?"

"Since nineteen-forty."

"That long? No wonder you want to go home."

"It isn't that I want to go. I should be in there doing my bit with the others."

"But aren't you awfully young, to fight, I mean?"

"I'll be eighteen soon."

"Oh." Jenifer wished she could find some other word for her replies to this strange boy, some word which would make him say why he stayed in America if he wanted so much to fight; but she could only stare at the drawings, and when she turned the last page he held out his hand for the book.

"I meant that about you having the sketch, you know," he said. "I'll have to be going now."

"Do you—do you live near here?"

"In the white house just behind you." He got slowly to his feet, and as she reached for the piece of paper on the ground between them she looked up to say:

"Thank you very much for the picture. I'll have it framed."

"It's really nothing. Thanks for posing. Good-by."

He walked across the street and, though he was very slight and not much taller than she was, Jenifer thought he belonged on such a driveway. She could even imagine him lounging morosely in the great rooms, his white face cold against a backdrop of red drapes as he listlessly took a cup of tea from a butler's silver tray.

"He was the queerest boy," she said to Peter after she had propped the sketch on the mantel. "I couldn't think of anything to say to him. It was like talking to a—to a whitewashed wall."

"Oh, I say, Jen," Peter mimicked, "rahlly old thing, I've never known you at a loss for words."

"Well, I was this time and you don't need to be silly." Jenifer dropped down on the divan and scowled at the picture. "I wish I knew more about him," she fumed. "Who he is and why he's here. Peter. . . ."

"Don't ask me to snoop for you. He's your little chum. I don't want him."

"But couldn't you ask around? Ask someone at school?"

"Hunhuh." Peter was pulling on a heavy turtle-neck sweater and he flailed his arms, mumbling as he wriggled into it, "You'd better pick up the kids. It's almost time for retreat and I have to feed my horse."

It was over a week before Jenifer saw the boy again. Even though she took Bitsy to feed the swans so often that the bread bill suffered. As soon as she and Bitsy appeared with their paper sack the swans turned back from any destination they might have, and the ducks and gulls and mud hens skimmed over the top of the water, aquaplaning to a stop. Bitsy threw her crumbs into the lake while Jenifer sat on a bench trying not to look behind her. And at last Bitsy said in rebellion:

"I think our own ducks are getting hungry. I think I'd rather stay home for a while and feed our own ducks."

After that, Jenifer walked to the grocery store the long way round in order to pass the house. She even hitched up Royal, who by now was fairly proficient in the art of carriage pulling, and drove him at a spanking trot around the little lake. But nothing happened. "The troublesome boy must have got himself to England after all," she decided, putting away her interest that was as tenacious as the Federal Bureau of Investigation. "Now I'll never find out what made his face so strange."

But she did find out, or at least she saw him again. After all the weary miles she had trudged, after all the wasted bread, she met him at her own front gate. She was sitting on Royal, one leg across the pommel of the saddle as she stretched to reach the mail box, when she saw him walking slowly along the lane. He carried a heavy stick with which he struck at stones in a one-handed game of golf, making little spurts of sand leap up. Jenifer slid back into the saddle, watched him stroll toward her, and when he was about to pass her, called:

"Hello."

"Oh, hello." He looked at her as if he were merely exchanging an afternoon greeting with a stranger and walked on. But when he was almost by he stopped. "I say, you're the girl who's picture I drew, aren't you?" he asked in surprise. And then before she could answer he crossed the road and laid his hand on Royal's neck. "That's a nice horse you have," he said.

"Yes, isn't he?" Jenifer prayed that Royal would know how important the moment was and stand still.

"I've got a horse, but not as nice as this one." He bent to slide his hand down the burnished-gold foreleg and Royal, who had very little sense, thought he was Peter and nipped him gently on the shoulder.

The boy straightened quickly and for just a second his eyes looked soft and he almost smiled.

"Would you like to ride him?" Jenifer asked.

"I don't think so, thanks."

"Please do." She was swinging to the ground while she talked. "I let you draw my picture," she said holding out the reins, "and I wish you'd ride my horse. I know you'd like him."

"I don't doubt it." The boy put his hands in his pockets, ignoring the proffered reins; not rudely but with a look of regret. "Sorry," he said. "I've ridden once this morning."

"But couldn't you ride again? Just up the road and back?"

"No. I only ride once a day." And then seeing her face grow puzzled he added reluctantly, as if the words were wrung from him, "It's doctor's orders. I want so very much to go home, you know."

"Oh I'm so sorry." Jenifer hung the reins over her arm and smiled at him. "I didn't know you were ill."

"I'm not, really. I just got a bit of the bombing in England. Those things take time, you know." He stepped back in the road and swished his stick in the dust, "It was nice seeing you again."

"And I'm awfully glad you happened by. You know," Jenifer confessed, pulling up Royal's head that was reaching for grass, "I've really been looking for you."

"You have?"

"Yes, I . . ." She hesitated, wondered if she dared, and then said bravely, "I didn't understand why it was, but I thought about you. You worried me. Just as Peter, he's my brother, just as Peter would worry me if . . . I can't explain it," she shrugged helplessly. "Perhaps I'm not very good at explaining my thoughts, but . . . won't you come and see us sometime?"

"Thank you." He stood stiffly in the roadway. All his friendliness was gone, leaving his eyes back in his burned-out face. "My days are rather full."

Jenifer watched him turn away. She stood leaning against Royal and watching him walk off down the road. She was a little angry at his rudeness but more furious with herself for the blunt delivery of her invitation. She knew something she had said had hurt him and she felt a great surge of pity for his thin shoulders under their expensive tailored jacket. When suddenly he stopped walking she straightened up, and when he faced around and came back toward her she took Royal by the bit and went to meet him.

"Would you care to ride tomorrow?" he asked, looking directly at her.

"I'd love to. At what time?"

"At ten. I always ride with my tutor—but I'd like to ride with you."

"All right. I'll be ready at ten." Jenifer knew nothing more to say so she turned Royal around and without another word they parted.

She had no time to wonder what his thoughts were on his homeward walk for she was too busy planning tomorrow's schedule.

"You'll have to take Bitsy to Mr. Cadwallader's on your way to school," she said to Peter who saw no sense to any of it. "I wouldn't trust her with Rosie, and I think I'll wear boots and breeches and I'll have to press my coat."

"You're crazy," Peter answered, dipping out a generous mug of oats for Royal, "to go riding with a boy when you don't even know his name."

"But I will tomorrow." Jenifer looked dreamy as she always did when she was plotting something. "After all," she said, sitting on a bale of hay and matching the tips of her thumbs together, "I already know he's got a tutor and was bombed in England. He only knows I have a brother and a horse."

CHAPTER VI

A GREAT deal of whispering was going on in the hall between the WAC's and the enlisted men's barracks.

"But surely you can give *something*, Vance," Gwenn was saying, fondly stroking the flat tissue-wrapped package she held. "Of course, it couldn't be as nice as what I'm giving, but you must have *something*."

Vance shook his head in anguish. "I haven't," he moaned. "I haven't a single thing that Jenifer would want."

"Oh, you have." Gwenn was losing patience with him. "Bitsy has, everybody has something but you. Go back and look again." She gave him a push and went off down the hall, walking on her toes with her hips swaying because she liked to feel her pleated skirt swing from side to side. "For goodness' sake, Alice," she called over her shoulder, "come *on!* Do you want to be late for breakfast and get extra k.p. again?"

Alice looked down once more at the package she held. It was a small knobby package done up in brown paper and tied in a hit-or-miss fashion with string. She was undecided whether to follow Gwenn or like Vance, go back for another search among her treasures. But Gwenn was calling again and Bitsy was dancing along the hall, so she held out her hand to Vance who sidled from his barracks concealing something behind him.

"What did you find, Vancey?" she asked as they raced along.

"Nothing."

"But you must have or you wouldn't come out."

71

"Hunhuh."

The others were already in the dining room and Jenifer was standing by her place at the table looking down at a pile of gifts.

"Well, what on earth!" she was saying as Alice dropped her package on the pile and Vance slid something underneath. "This isn't my birthday, so what's it all about?"

"They're presents for you to wear on your ride," Gwenn explained importantly. "I thought of it because we want you to look nice when you go out with the Englishman."

"Why, darlings!" Jenifer picked up a package. It was the fancy one in tissue paper and Gwenn hung over the back of a chair to watch her open it. "Oh, Gwenn, it's your stock!" Jenifer exclaimed. "the one you wore when you rode in the horse show at Fort Riley. Darling, thank you, but I simply couldn't take it."

"I want you to have it," Gwenn said, tossing back her curls as if bestowing a large part of her kingdom on a pauper prince. "It will be stunning with your habit and you'll simply knock him dead."

"Well . . ." Jenifer's hands moved on. There was a bright red ribbon from Bitsy, Peter's favorite crop, Donny's spurs with only a little of the nickel off, a handkerchief that had once been white, from Neal, and Susan had offered her Crabapple toilet water, and Alice her woven Indian belt. Vance's donation still lay like a round black spot on the table and Jenifer looked at it and laughed.

"Why the compass, Vancey?" she asked. "Did you think I might get lost in Orlando?"

"It was all I could find," Vance mumbled, digging his

toe into the carpet and blushing under all the eyes. "I had to give you that or my turtle and I didn't think the turtle ought to stay out of his tank so long."

"Well the compass is fine." Jenifer frowned at the snickers and giggles. "I may get turned around in my directions," she said, "and be glad I have it in my pocket."

"Except . . ." Vance flashed his eyes upward and down again. "It doesn't work so good," he admitted. "It's busted.

"Oh, that won't matter." Jenifer picked up the compass and watched its needle jump around like a frightened hen trying to find a place to roost. "I'll just pretend it works," she said. "And thank you, darlings, all of you."

"And see that you get home with my crop," Peter mentioned. "It's only a loan."

"Indian giver," Jenifer laughed. She held the crop over him and touched him lightly on the shoulder with it. "I hereby dub you Knight of the Indian Giver," she said solemnly. "Fall to, oh Knight, and quaff your breakfast, that Her Royal Highness may array herself in queenly raiment to sally forth on her steed through the ancestral forests. I pray ye, eat."

"Can I be something too, Jenifer?" Gwenn coaxed, holding out her hand as if expecting to have it kissed. "Lady Gwendolyn in-waiting or something?"

"Or something," Jenifer answered, smacking Gwenn's hand with the crop. "You can be just what you always are, enlisted personnel." She carried her gifts to the buffet and said into the mirror above it, "Eat, men, so you can clear the table and make the bus. And thanks for my loot."

She laughed a great deal while she was dressing to go for her ride; and since it wouldn't have occurred to her to leave off a single one of the items spread on her bed she had quite a time. Donny's spurs were too small and she bent them wider and tugged the straps over her boots. Bitsy's ribbon that tied her hair into a pony tail ill became the formality of Gwenn's stock, and the cleanest corner of the perfume-drenched handkerchief protruded grayly from her breast pocket. She anchored her breeches with Alice's belt, feeling bound by a life preserver, and dropped the useless compass into her pocket. She whistled joyously while she dressed, dwelling tenderly on the donors of the terrible gifts, and hoping Royal wouldn't mind the rowels on her spurs, or the English boy her asphyxiating scent.

When she was ready she loped janglingly across the lawn and pulled Royal out of his stall. Peter had rubbed him until he had a brighter polish than Jenifer's boots and the sun on his buckles and bits was blinding. She led him out to the gate where she stood feeding him a carrot and, since it was almost ten o'clock, carefully wiping his mouth with a wad of dried grass.

Inside the house a clock chimed softly. In fifteen minutes it played a quarter tune; and when Royal was nibbling at the lawn with Jenifer not caring how much green foam he left on his bit, it added a few more notes and struck one soft reminder that half an hour had passed.

"Uhuh, you got stood up," Jenifer said to Royal. "Let this be a lesson to you—never make dates with strange horses."

A colored man was ambling down the road. He seemed to be taking a nap between steps but when he reached Jenifer he rolled his eyes toward her and asked:

"Is yo' 'spectin' to go ridin' with Mistah Cyril? Is yo'?"

"Well," Jenifer jerked up Royal's head and walked across the road. "I was expecting to go riding with some-one," she said. "I didn't know his name was Cyril."

"Well, he ain't comin'. Miz Van Courtlandt say he's sick."

"Oh, I'm sorry."

"But *he* say," the colored man took off his hat and scratched his head thoughtfully, "he say what's yo' name so he can telephone yo'?"

"It's Jenifer Jordon. Jordon. And the telephone number is two, three-one-five-five. Can you remember that?"

"Yes'm. Jordon. I got ways of rememberin'."

He wandered back the way he had come and Jenifer gathered up her reins and mounted Royal. "We might as well go pick up Bitsy," she told him, letting him find his way along the lane while she took off Gwenn's stock and put it carefully in her pocket.

Mr. Cadwallader lived with Lacey in a small white cottage that hugged the store, and when Jenifer tied Royal to a fence that separated the dusty parking lot from his neat back yard he waved to her from his office window.

"Bitsy's over to the house havin' cookies and milk with the hired girl," he shouted. "Come in here, Jenifer."

She ran up the steep wooden steps that led into his storeroom, and when she looked around the door into his office he lowered the shade against the sun and asked belligerently, "What in tarnation do you mean, goin' out ridin' with some boy you never heard of?"

Jenifer laughed and sat on the edge of his desk while she explained to him. "Oh," he said when she had finished, "so that's it. I thought from what Bitsy managed to say that you'd gone straight to perdition. What kind of a boy is he?"

Jenifer tried to tell him what she knew but he pushed her roughly off the desk and began to fuss with his papers. "Rich, huh," he muttered. "I reckon he's too danged rich to keep a promise. Just for that I've a good notion not to let that woman have any butter this week."

"Do you know Mrs. Van Courtlandt?" Jenifer asked, guessing whom he meant.

"Know her?" Mr. Cadwallader snorted. "I know her cook's voice on the telephone and her chauffeur that comes for the groceries. And I've seen the boy too. They're society folks, Jenifer, high society; and I wouldn't doubt that that boy's a second Lord Fauntleroy—kin to an earl or somethin'."

Jenifer began to laugh. She laughed so hard she had to wipe her eyes with Neal's handkerchief; and Mr. Cadwallader was secretly pleased to think he had caused such peals of merriment. But he only gave an inkwell a shove and looked at her over his glasses. "Stop that silliness," he growled. "Lacey's comin' over to stay with you."

"Lacey is not."

"She's comin'. She's bringin' her traps tonight."

"Oh, Mr. Cadwallader." Jenifer stopped laughing and her eyes grew soft as she looked at his round face with its fine criss-cross of wrinkles. "I haven't room for Lacey. She wouldn't have a place. . . ."

"Well, she's bringin' *half* her traps. She kin fluctuate between here an' there. When that boy comes to see you she kin act as hostess, can't she?"

"It doesn't look as if he's coming."

"He'll be there. When a young girl's as pretty as you are boys find the way, and there's got to be a hostess to receive 'em."

"No one receives Andy."

"He don't matter. He's too old fer you. You're all just kids to him." Mr. Cadwallader heard the store bell tinkle as someone opened the door and he called as he hurried out, "Think about what I said, Jenifer. Lacey's comin'."

Jenifer thought about it all the way home with Bitsy perched on the saddle in front of her. It would be fun to have Lacey always in the house, but she sighed and shook her head.

The telephone was ringing when she came in from putting up Royal and as she ran for it she saw Rosie clutch the receiver. "No one lives here by that name," Rosie was saying when Jenifer reached her. "What? Sure, I'm sure. I never heard the name before."

"Give me the phone," Jenifer said, reaching out. "Perhaps I can understand." When Rosie reluctantly released the receiver she put it to her ear and heard the clipped sentences of the boy named Cyril.

"But there must be a Miss River there," he was saying. "I want to speak to Miss River Jordon."

For the second time that day Jenifer needed Neal's

handkerchief. She crumpled it over her mouth this time until she could swallow her mirth and say carefully, "This is Jenifer Jordon. I think. . . ." But it was no use. She went off into a gale of laughter.

"Please," she managed to gasp, "don't hang up. I'm —Jenifer."

"Oh." There was magic in the word now, since he had been forced to use it, and she hooked a chair with her foot and sat down with the phone.

"I'm the girl you were to ride with," she said, swallowing hard but still grinning broadly. "You see, I told the colored man my name was Jordon and asked him if he could remember it. He said he had 'ways,' and so. . . ."

"The river Jordon. I get it. Not bad."

"I knew a Ford Carr once."

"And I heard, just the other day, of a Pearl Button."

"But I'm not a River."

They laughed together now and Jenifer thought he had a nice laugh and should use it more often.

"Sorry about this morning," he said. "I could have ridden but Aunt Kate gets in such a stew."

So the "high society" woman was his aunt, Jenifer thought, listening to him.

"Could I come over and explain?"

"Please do."

"This afternoon about three? Right?"

"Righto."

"Oh, my soul, I'm going British," Jenifer muttered in dismay, rushing out to the kitchen to peer into the cake box. "What is there about that boy that mixes me up so? And why did I say three o'clock was all right? It isn't all right. There'll be millions of kids coming home. And Bitsy'll be up from her nap and Rosie has ironing to do . . . oh dear."

She forgot what she had seen in the cake box, so she looked again and followed it up with a search of the pantry shelves for a sandwich spread. "I do hope he won't have another attack," she told the can opener, working it violently around a tin of potted ham. "If he doesn't show up this time . . ." She gave the can a shove that skidded it across the table and decided suddenly:

"I won't give him tea. I got all ready for him once and I'm not going to do it again. He can just take the kids and like 'em. And if I look funny without a hostess . . . I look funny without a hostess. So what? And furthermore," she said, preparing to use the ham in a large thick sandwich for herself, "Mr. Cyril Whatever-your-name-is, kin to an earl, you can dang well come or not—just as you please."

CHAPTER VII

WHEN three o'clock came Jenifer refused to sit in the living room and wait for the doorbell to ring. She had changed from her riding clothes to a blue print dress and her hair hung in its customary tan cloud about her shoulders. Bitsy's ribbon had been folded and returned to the candy box in which she kept it, and when the other donations were back in their places Jenifer wandered out to the kitchen.

The clock on the stove was ticking merrily as if gloating over the way it pushed its hands along, but she refused even to glance at it. She took a cooky from the cake box and strolling to the back door said to herself, "If I had anything else to do I'd go do it. I certainly wouldn't wait. . . ." And then she looked down. Cyril was sitting on the back steps. His legs were crossed and with his elbow on his knee, his chin resting in the palm of his hand, he looked as if he had been there a long time.

"Well!" Jenifer exclaimed, almost choking on her cooky.

"Hello." He turned to look at her and his thin cheek slid into his hand. "It's beautiful out here," he answered, pulling himself back from some far place. "It's so beautifully peaceful." And then he jumped up. "Sorry," he said, "I meant to knock, and then I saw the lake and walked around to have a look at it."

"That's all right." Jenifer came down the steps and asked, "Would you like to sit on the boathouse deck?"

"Yes." He turned and began walking away, and hurrying to keep up with him she thought:

He's an arrogant piece. Maybe Mr. Cadwallader knows what he's talking about. But she only said cheerfully, "It seems peaceful here now but wait till the children come home. You'll think you've got in a circus then."

"The children?"

"My brothers and sisters."

Cyril stopped. He looked at Jenifer in startled silence, at the lake, and back at Jenifer again. "If you don't mind," he said, thrusting clenched fists into the pockets of his jacket, "I think I'll apologize for this morning and run along. I'm really rather. . . ."

"Is it because of the children?" Jenifer too stopped and there was a little frown between her eyes. "Don't you like children?"

"Yes, very much, but . . ." The boy jerked out a hand to smooth back his hair. "I used to like children—I don't know any now, of course . . ." He was struggling with some secret emotion and Jenifer forgot her irritation in a desire to help him. She was searching for words when he muttered, "Would you mind taking a walk down the road?"

"Of course not. I'd love to."

They walked around the house together and when they were in the sandy lane she heard him sigh and saw him scrub at his forehead with his fingers.

"You have a headache, haven't you?" she asked. "Perhaps you shouldn't have come."

"Oh no. It's nothing, really. I wanted very much to come."

They walked on in silence until they reached a large

wooded lot that bordered the lake and without a word Jenifer followed him into it, their shoes as silent in the sandy soil as they were. Giant pines had shed their needles in small scatter rugs on a lush green carpet, and near the water a live oak tree spread its branches into a circular room.

"This is where I often come," the boy said, standing close to the tree and resting his hand against its great trunk. "You're the first person I've shown it to."

"I like it." Jenifer dropped down on the grass under the tree and said, with her eyes on the lake, "It's good to be alone sometimes—but not too much. Cyril . . ." she turned her head to look up at him and to ask, "your name *is* Cyril, isn't it?" And at his nod went on, "Do you *always* like to be alone?"

"I hate it!"

He jerked his hand away from the tree and his shoulders drooped as if he had torn loose from a current of strength that flowed from the tree into his tired body.

"Then why. . . ."

"Because it's better than being with people."

He stared moodily into the distance and Jenifer, fearing he might turn on his heel and leave her, ignored his words and said lightly, "Come over here and sit down and let's talk. We've never really talked to each other."

"About what?"

"Oh, about things we think and things we like to do." She laughed and quoted softly, " 'Of ships and shoes and sealing wax, of cabbages and kings.' We have lots to talk about."

"Very well, fire away." He threw himself on the ground beside her and pillowed his head on his arm. "What you really want to talk about is me, isn't it? Like everyone else, you want to know why I'm such a disgusting chap."

"No." Jenifer shook her head. "I'm not a bit concerned with you being, as you say, a 'disgusting chap'; or, as we say, a mess—because I don't think you are. I think you're suffering from some very real trouble and I wish I could help you." He made no answer so she went on, "But since I can't, because I don't know what's wrong, I'd just as soon talk of something pleasant."

"I don't know anything pleasant to talk of."

"Well, I do." She began telling him about the children and about her father overseas. He lay listening to her, his dark eyes never wavering from hers, his tense mouth slowly relaxing.

"Why do you want to drive Royal?" he asked when she had finished her description of Royal's first venture with the carriage.

"Because we can get around better. He'll be no end of help."

"I had a pony once, and a basket cart," he said dreamily, almost as if he had forgotten she was there. "Nanny used to take Alfred and Lolly and me out in it. Alfred always drove and Lolly sat in the back and I had to sit on Nanny's lap."

"Who's Alfred?"

"He was my brother."

He rolled over and buried his face in his arms and Jenifer leaned forward to lay her hand on his shoulder.

"Was he killed in the war, Cyril? Is that what hurts so much?"

"Yes." The boy lifted his head and his dark eyes looked into hers in black torture. "He was killed and I wasn't. I should have been the one who was killed."

"Cyril." Jenifer's hand still held his shoulder and their faces were close together. "Try to tell me a little more," she coaxed, "and please believe me when I say that if you can talk things over with someone your own age it helps a lot. I can't be friends with you, Cyril, when I don't know what you're thinking. And I want very much to be friends."

He looked at her for a long moment then raised himself on his elbow and turned his face away from her to the lake. "I've thought of you as a friend," he said slowly. "I thought of you almost all last night, just as I think so many nights of Lolly . . . because you are sweet. And again on the phone today you were like Lolly when she chattered nonsense with boys." His lip caught between his teeth and he looked down at his fist that was pressed against the hard ground. "I almost thought you *were* Lolly," he muttered.

"Lolly would know how to help you, wouldn't she, Cyril?"

"She'd try. But no one can do any good."

"Then let me try. Let me share things with you as Lolly would."

She waited a long time for his answer and when it came it was so different from what she had expected that she sat up straighter.

"I grew up in the country," he said, as if having made up his mind to explain himself he wanted to get it over quickly, "although we spent bits of the year in London. My father is Lord Carlington, and there were Mum and Alfred, then Lolly, then me. Alfred was always the leader. When boys came to stay with us he always beat them at games and when he was sent away to school he brought home all the honors in his form. He was never afraid, as I was. When I went off to school I was so slow that my marks were always poor and the masters who had had Alfred were disappointed in me."

Jenifer could see the little boy who struggled to follow an older brother, trying to be good at games, trying to reach through his shyness to his teachers; but his voice was going on in almost a monotone, as if he had repeated the story to himself many times.

"Lolly didn't care if she were good at lessons or not. She had a governess who let her study what she pleased and she could best my father in a political argument, and speak beautiful French, and could read Greek. My father adored Lolly. Once she struck him because he took away my brushes and paints, but he only laughed at her and gave the paints back. And then he glowered at me and said he was glad Alfred was the older son."

"Alfred would have inherited the estates and title, wouldn't he?" Jenifer asked, hoping not to disturb him.

"Yes, he should have. That's why it's so bad, you see. Father was so proud of Alfred, and . . . and no matter how hard he tried he never could be proud of me."

"Oh, but Cyril, he was, he *is*. You were such a little boy then."

"No, only Mum was proud. We used to take long walks through the woods and she would sit quite still for hours while I painted. She liked for me to paint and she was going to have me take lessons when the war came on.

"Alfred was twenty then, and he joined up right away and was given a commission in the Air Force. He was a wonderful flier. I saw him fly once." Cyril sat up and clasped his hands around his knees and Jenifer watched his face light up as he looked into the sky. "His plane . . . his plane was like a great hawk that swooped down, then soared away and came back to swoop again. I could imagine Alfred smiling when he swooped and soared and made his plane do all the things he wanted it to do."

"Was he killed flying a mission?" Jenifer asked softly.

"No." Cyril rested one arm on his knees and pressed his forehead against his wrist. "This is the part that's so hard to tell," he said, rubbing his forehead back and forth across his wrist. "The first part was so easy, Jenifer, compared to this."

"Don't tell it then, Cyril, don't even try to remember it. You've told me enough so I can understand."

"But I must tell you, now that I've started. You see . . ." He sighed, then lifted his head and turned to face her, "Alfred got leave," he said, his voice quite steady, "not enough leave to come home to the country, just overnight, so that Mum was going up to London to meet him. Lolly and I begged so hard to go with her that finally, although my father didn't want us to go, she took us. We met Alfred and had dinner at Claridge's and it was all very jolly. He was handsome in his uniform, blond and big and tall, and he teased Mum and said he couldn't tell her and Lolly apart, and slipped me some notes so I could pay the dinner check. Alfred had brought along an air cadet for Lolly who was just seventeen, and I was feeling very important and quite the man of the world because I had never dined out so late before."

He moistened his dry lips, then took a deep breath and leaned a little toward her. "When we came out of the restaurant to go back to the flat we always kept in London it was as dark as a pocket and there wasn't a cab to be had. Mum thought she would like to walk a little way until we could pick up a cab, and I was happy to have the evening last a little longer. So we started out, with Lolly in front between the cadet and Alfred, and Mum and I walking behind, with her arm tucked through mine. That was when she told me I was to have a tutor and not go back to school.

" 'I need you at home, Cyril,' she said. 'The house is too lonely without you.' I'll always remember the way she said that and gave my arm a little squeeze—for then the sirens went off. There was a shelter only a block or so away and we began to run with the crowd. Wardens were clearing the streets and people were bumping into us. Alfred had Lolly by the hand and Mum and I were right behind them. And then, because I was always so clumsy, I stumbled and fell on the curb. I was clinging to Mum and the others ran on. Mum . . . Mum and I. . . ."

His hands were twisting together and Jenifer, reaching out to touch them, found them cold and wet. "Please, Cyril, don't go on," she begged, "I know what happened."

"But I have to go on. I always have to go on when I get this far. I have to go on . . . wherever I am. . . ."

He was breathing heavily like a person in a nightmare and Jenifer knelt beside him and gripped his hands tightly in hers. "Cyril dear, let me finish it for you, quickly," she whispered. "Alfred and Lolly are gone and you and your mother are left. That's it, isn't it?"

"Yes."

"And you're here with your aunt, getting well and strong, and someday you're going back to take over."

"But Alfred—even when I'm well and strong enough to fight, I can't . . . I can't take Alfred's place, not with Mum and my father."

"You don't want to take Alfred's place. You have your own, Cyril. That's what you must always remember and plan for. You aren't like Alfred, you aren't like Lolly. You're Cyril. There's a great deal to live up to, being Cyril."

"I'll never be able to do it, Jenifer. I don't want to and I never will."

"Of course you will." Jenifer released his hands and sat back on her heels. "Look," she said, drawing his eyes up to hers. "I'm Jenifer, and I have to be a good Jenifer. It's uphill work sometimes but I have to keep at it. And you do, too."

He turned his face away but she reached out to touch his cheek and bring him back to her. "I mean it, Cyril," she told him. "You can't live in the past and build a future. We're friends. Cyril and Jenifer. And I'm not going to let you stay in the past. Would you *want* me to? Is that all you want of my friendship, just to have me feel sorry for you?"

"No."

"Then we won't talk about it anymore. We'll talk of your family, lots, and we'll remember the things you did that were fun, but we won't talk about the part that hurts. It's gone and we'll let it stay gone. Will you do that?"

"I'll try."

"Then it's as good as done." For a moment she considered saying more and then announced lightly, "And now I have to get home for retreat. Would you like to come with me?"

"Not this evening."

"Cyril!" Jenifer was getting up but she stopped on one knee and looked at him reproachfully. "You're hiding again," she admonished.

"No, I'm not, really. I can't come because I haven't told Aunt Kate and she likes me to have tea with her."

"All right, then I'll let you off this time." She held out her hand and he scrambled to his feet and pulled her up. "But Aunt Kate will have to get used to doing without you," she said. "Is she your real aunt or just someone you were sent to stay with?"

"She's my mother's sister. After the doctors had patched me up my father sent me over to her. Mum is an American too."

"Um, how nice." Jenifer swung his hand in hers as they

walked along the lane. "Americans have a lot of grit and determination," she said with a lift of her head. "Daddy calls it stick-to-it-ive-ness. And I'm glad you have some of it."

At her gate she lingered even though Peter was blowing the saxophone. "Remember," she cautioned, "no thinking tonight. Promise?"

"I promise."

"And a glass of hot milk before you go to bed, so you'll sleep?"

"Right."

"And Cyril," Jenifer leaned closer to him and grinned, "when you come over, for you *are* coming over, don't mind if the children stare at you. You see, they've never known a boy who's going to be a real live lord someday."

She gave his hand a squeeze and went racing along the drive, calling good-by and waving first to him and then to Peter, not knowing that his eyes followed her hopefully and that he held his thin shoulders a little straighter.

CHAPTER VIII

"AS I told Cyril, stick-to-it-ive-ness is a very good thing to have," Jenifer said, sitting cross-legged and looking at Andy who was sprawled on the boathouse deck listening to her recital of her talk with Cyril, "but I think his aunt has too much of it. Listen to this note she sent me. It sounds friendly, but it isn't." She fished a piece of expensive stationery from her dirndl pocket and spread it out on her knee to read. " 'Dear Miss Jordon: Cyril has told me of knowing you, of what a help you have been to him, and I welcome anything that will lift the dear boy out of his trouble.' ('Anything' means me,)" Jenifer interpreted before rushing on. " 'So won't you have tea with me on Thursday, at four? Sincerely, Katherine Hoyt Van Courtlandt.' See what I mean?"

"Yep."

She's kept Cyril at home all yesterday and today, when if she really wanted to help him she'd say, 'now run along and see that nice girl all you can.' But does she?"

"Nope."

"She just invites me to the mausoleum. No one, not even I, can be bright and cheery in a mausoleum with a cup of tea in one hand and bits of this and that in the other."

"She needs a kick in the teeth." Andy squinted into the setting sun that was a round red ball across the lake. "Why don't you buy Rosie a uniform and a cap and send her over with regrets?" he suggested.

"Because I'm going to tea. I telephoned Cyril I'd come.

Just nice and friendly, like I'd be with any boy whose mother had invited me. Poor lamb, he was so happy about it."

"Maybe he thinks the old girl has his interest at heart."

"I don't doubt he does. And perhaps she has, Andy." Jenifer folded up the letter and tucked it away. "Perhaps she just doesn't understand boys. And of course she's scared stiff about him; he isn't hers, you know, and he has to go back to inherit the title. Well . . ." She got up and grinned down at him. Andy was such a satisfying companion; so completely relaxed when he wanted to be lazy and tuned to the power of one of his plane motors when he was in action. "Do you ever let the war get you down, Andy?" she asked curiously. "You only tell us about the funny things that happened to you in England."

"Why tell the others? What I felt or suffered on a bombing raid couldn't possibly be felt or suffered by anyone but me. I couldn't explain it, you couldn't understand it, so why not let the writers and correspondents tell of the horrors? They've got the words to do it; and the horrors are there all right, but I've got to go back and I'd just as soon take a lot of happy memories with me. Do you reckon my gal Lacey has come yet?"

"Not yet. She said she'd be late because she's going by home to pick up a meat loaf."

"Well, tell her I'll see her down here in my office."

"Lacey won't like that."

"She won't at that, will she?" Andy got up and twisted around to brush the dust from his uniform. "Lacey is a very stubborn girl," he said ruefully.

He followed Jenifer up the path but detoured to poke his head in the stable door. Peter was watering Royal from a bucket and Alice, in a pair of faded overalls, was pitching bedding into the stall. "Well, Sweet Little Alice Blue Gown," Andy said, leaning against the door, "what do you think you are?"

"A week's stable orderly," Alice answered, spreading the straw with a pitchfork.

"For climbing again?"

"Hunhuh. Poor grades."

"I don't know how this place would run without you," Andy laughed. "Your name takes up more space on the bulletin board than any kid's in the bunch. Do you *try* to do everything wrong?"

"I don't have to try; it's a gift."

Alice stooped down to smooth out a lump in the straw and Peter said gruffly, "That's good enough, you aren't icing a cake. Now you can saddle soap the harness and you'd better turn on the light in the tack room."

"Is she going to be here till dark?" Andy asked when Alice had gone. "Poor kid, won't she eat?"

"Oh, she'll eat." Peter unsnapped the rope from Royal's halter and let him go into his stall. He reached inside to set the bucket of water in a box nailed to the wall and closed the gate. "So long, Alice," he called. "I'll send Donny out to help you."

Only a rattle of bits came from the tack room and as he walked up the path Peter boasted to Andy, "She'll do a good job."

Lacey was in the kitchen, unpacking the meat loaf. She

set the pan in the warming oven and looked up in well-feigned surprise when Andy came in. "Well, fancy seeing you here."

"Well, fancy *not* seeing me here." He tossed his cap on the table and straddled a chair. "Hello, beautiful one," he said. "Long time no see. Ten hours."

"Only that long?" Lacey picked up his cap and carried it into the hall and Andy stuck out his crooked lower lip and said loudly to Peter:

"She's jealous. She's jealous because you're all fonder of me." And then he lowered his voice and asked anxiously, "Do you suppose she'll come back?"

Peter shrugged and went off to find Donny, and much to Andy's surprise Lacey did come back.

"Rosie has a toothache," she said, dumping a green mountain of beans into the sink. "Gwenn and Neal are on the roster to help but. . . ."

"I'll be Rosie." Andy hitched his chair close to the sink and crossed his knees. "Rosie never was much good," he remarked, searching in his pockets for a cigarette. Then at Lacey's nod toward the closed door he leaned forward to whisper, "I've always wanted to be someone as dumb and carefree as Rosie."

"Well, I don't know about the carefree part," Lacey said, looking at him through her eyelashes in a way that always ruined Andy's repartee, "but you'd better move over if you don't want to be splashed."

He slid grudgingly back and Lacey gave him a bean to string. He absentmindedly bit off its end and sat chewing

thoughtfully while he watched her hands swirling the
beans around in a pan of cold water.

"How long have I known you?" he asked.

"Five weeks." Lacey turned off the water and began to
snap the beans, dropping them with little plops into a
kettle.

"Do you ever worry about the kids?"

"All the time. Why do you think I'm here so much?"

"I'd hoped it was because I'm here so much too."

"Oh, you fit into the picture." Lacey looked intently at
a bean that had rust on it, then dropped it back in the sink.
She went on snapping, tossing a handful into the kettle,
and snapping again, while Andy watched her. She looked
like a little girl bending over the sink, her long lashes
lying on her cheeks and her mouth puckered in concen-
tration, and Andy leaned forward.

"Aunt Lacey," he said suddenly, "will you marry me?"

"I should say not, my dear Uncle Andy." Her reply was
prompt, but he argued:

"We could live here and take care of the children."

"I practically live here now," Lacey said, "and nine
children are enough. One more. . . ."

"But this one would help you."

"Just like you're helping now, I suppose." Lacey picked
up her kettle of beans and took them to the stove. "Thank
you, my good man," she said, "but I'll take Rosie."

"Aw, Lacey."

"What's Lacey done?"

Jenifer asked the question from the dining room door at

a most inopportune moment, and when Andy answered, "Nothing, for once," Lacey sighed. Such a good plot ruined, she thought, flipping on the gas. Like an exciting serial that, when it reaches a climax, has "continued" written at the bottom of the page.

She was a little ashamed of the thought, for Jenifer had rushed to the potato bin and was pawing into a burlap bag. "I'm sorry not to have been out here to help," she cried, "but Donny was all tied up in knots over an arithmetic problem."

"Hasn't Donny gone out to help Alice?" asked Andy.

"No, he's untying himself."

Gwenn had come dancing in, her curls piled on top of her head, her mouth smeared with lipstick, and she was whisking about airily hoping someone would notice her. Andy did. He turned sidewise on his chair and rested his arms on its back.

"What have *you* been doing?" he asked.

"Putting up my hair and trying on Lacey's fox jacket." Gwenn stopped in the middle of the floor and pushed her curls higher. "Like it this way, Andy?" she asked, tilting her head at him.

"Why aren't **you** out helping Alice, when Donny couldn't go?"

"Well, *Andy!*" Gwenn had never seen Andy look stern before and she said plaintively, "After all, *I* got good marks. If Alice has to rub harness. . . ."

"Who helped you last week when you were tied up with a vacuum cleaning job and wouldn't have got to Scouts on time?"

"Why. . . ."

"You're darned right—Alice. And who took your turn with the dishes on Monday? Alice again. Now you get out to the barn and get there fast."

Gwenn's hands dropped from her hair and her blue eyes blazed. She threw back her head and stared at him, her mouth drawn into a tight hard line.

"That's an order from a superior officer, Gwenn," Andy said quietly, but with his gaze as straight as hers. "Now get going."

For a fraction of an instant Gwenn stood meeting his eyes then she whirled and ran out the back door, slamming it behind her.

"You're right, Andy," Jenifer nodded, kneeling with the potatoes in her lap. "We must never let consideration and tenderness slip, even in duty."

"Gwenn isn't considerate," he answered. "She's the only one in the bunch who isn't. She's pretty and clever, and selfish. Alice couldn't have stood it to be in here, with Gwenn out in the dark alone."

"No, she couldn't. And thanks for pointing it out."

"Okay." Andy turned in his chair to watch Lacey who had come back to the sink. His grin was wide again as he looked up at her, for Lacey had given his shoulder a pat as she passed it.

CHAPTER IX

JENIFER held her cup of tea and listened to Mrs. Van Courtlandt. There was nothing else she could do since Mrs. Van Courtlandt never stopped talking. She was a small woman with dazzling white teeth that looked strong enough to bite a tenpenny nail in two and her eyes were as dark as Cyril's but as keen as an X-ray machine. She wore a rose wool dress and her hair was brushed up smoothly on her head, and her little hands, on which diamond rings twinkled, handled the tea cups as if they dared them to break.

It was not a gay company that was having tea in the dark austere drawing room and Jenifer, who had seen into a bright sunroom, wished they could pick up their individual tables and move out around its fountain that gurgled in a jolly way. Cyril's tutor sat stiffly on a needlepoint sofa, and thick glasses astride a small patient nose told why he was not in uniform. He had a way of leaning forward to listen that was pathetically eager and although his pale hair was limp Jenifer liked him.

As for Cyril, she wanted to slap him. He had dug himself into an overstuffed chair and sat munching a cup cake and silently watching his aunt.

"I do think our dear boy looks better," Mrs. Van Courtlandt was saying, having disposed of the business of tea making, "don't you, Barry?"

"Yes, I certainly do." The young tutor leaned still farther forward, but she had already turned away from him and was explaining brightly to Jenifer, "Mr. MacDonald has been a wonderful help to Cyril. His devotion is so tireless and he follows the doctor's orders so carefully. I believe you have sisters and brothers, Miss Jordon, so you will know how anxious I feel."

"Yes, I have eight." Jenifer wedged the sentence in proudly but Mrs. Van Courtlandt looked slightly taken aback.

"Eight," she said. "Just fancy."

Her X-ray eyes bored through Jenifer and finding nothing they wished to record shot on to the impeccable butler who was passing the cakes again.

"No, darling!" she cried to Cyril who was reaching out for a cake. "I'm afraid you won't touch your dinner if you eat too much now."

Cyril's hand hovered over the plate and Jenifer thought she detected a hopeful look in the butler's eye. She wished he would push the plate into Cyril's stomach and say, "Here, take one," but he only waited impassively until Cyril withdrew his hand, then passed on.

"Thank you, dear boy," Mrs. Van Courtlandt said, smiling her porcelain smile.

Jenifer took a cake. She took it with determined casualness as if she were accustomed to eating a dozen cakes before dinner.

"It must be quite a trial having so many children to care for," Katherine Van Courtlandt remarked, continuing the conversation as if there had been no interruption, "to keep them well, at least."

"Oh, they're always well." Jenifer set her plate carefully on her little table and laid her napkin beside it. "We haven't time even for colds at our house."

"I imagine you haven't." Her hostess turned away and exclaimed, "Wouldn't it be wonderful, Barry, never to worry over illness? I can't think of anything quite so divine, can you?"

The young tutor had just taken a bite and he dropped his half-eaten cake on his plate trying to shake his head over a hasty swallow of tea while Mrs. Van Courtlandt tactfully ignored him and said to Cyril, "Reach out and ring for Simpson to take the tea things, darling. If you're all quite finished, that is."

There were no denials and while Cyril jabbed at a bell on the table beside him Jenifer stood up. "I should be at home now," she said. "We have retreat at five."

"Oh, must you . . ." Katherine Van Courtlandt cut off her sentence to send a vexed look at Cyril who had risen and was stalking silently toward the door. "It was sweet of you to come," she added with a frown, taking the firm hand Jenifer thrust out. "You must come again and cheer up our boy."

"Thank you. It was nice of you to have me today." Jenifer withdrew her hand and smiled good-by to Barry, then walked the length of the room to Cyril who waited by the door.

"Thank you, Cyril," she said, her chin higher than usual and two spots of color flaming in her cheeks.

"I'll walk up the lane with you."

He was about to slip through the door with her when

his aunt called gently, "No, darling. You must rest before dinner, you know."

"Yes," Jenifer said in a voice too low for the others to hear, "be sure to remember your rest." Then she added too loudly and all in a rush, "I've got to run, Cyril. Good-by."

She dashed across the wide hall and out the door, and as she ran down the steps she half hoped he would have enough courage to follow her. But she heard Simpson close the door and muttered fiercely to herself, "Hurry and lock it, before he gets in a draft."

Andy, Lacey, and Peter were sitting on the front steps when she got home and as her head appeared above the shrubbery that banked the fence Lacey called, "Come on, and tell us about it."

Jenifer marched across the grass, her color still high, and sat down on the step below them. "It was absolutely unbelievable," she said, looking up. "When I tell it you won't believe I'm telling the truth, but I am. I've never been in such a place, I've never seen such peculiar people, I've never been so mad, so disgusted, so. . . ."

"Well, spare us your reactions," Andy interrupted. "We can see those for ourselves. Give us a chance to have some."

"All right." Jenifer slammed her best purse on the step beside her and glared down at it with her lips pressed into such a straight line that her cheeks puffed out. "I don't think I ever want to show my teeth again," she said suddenly. "I've looked at such a fine set of teeth for an hour that. . . ."

"Listen, Red Ridinghood," Andy began, but Jenifer whirled around and cried:

"That's exactly what she is. The wolf. The wolf that says so-o sweetly, 'the better to eat you with, my dear.' Only she says 'my dear boy.'"

"Are you going to tell us or not?" Peter asked, giving her a poke with the saxophone. "We postponed retreat until five-thirty. You've got ten minutes."

"All right, this is the way it was." Jenifer slid up a step and began recounting the story of her afternoon. "Barry MacDonald was kind of sweet," she said when she had finished. "He's sort of a yes-man but what else could you expect? Cyril's the one who's a washout."

"He sounds like a droop to me." Peter picked up his saxophone, stood up, and with a hand on Jenifer's shoulder vaulted the steps to the ground.

"But what can the poor kid do, Jen?" Lacey asked, shaking her head. "He hasn't a chance."

"He can shout 'yes, I want another piece of cake.'"

"And be dosed with pills and a hot-water bottle all night, I suppose. Perhaps he was afraid his aunt would make a scene before you. Really, honey, I don't think he can openly rebel."

"Well, he should." The phone in the hall was ringing and she scrambled past Lacey to answer it. The others went on talking but straining to hear what she said, and when she had hung up the receiver she stood in the door and said in surprise, "Well! That was Cyril."

"Oh no!" Andy grinned up at her and she nodded and called down to Peter who was giving a few practice toots:

"He wants to know if I'll meet him up the lane. Could I be excused from retreat, just this once? I want to hear what he has to say for himself."

"Okay, this once. But how do you suppose he sneaked out?"

"Through a basement window probably." Jenifer was already starting down the steps. "Don't go away, Lacey or Andy," she said. "Tell Rosie to bake a couple of extra potatoes and we'll whip up a salad when I come back."

"Bring Cyril home with you, I want to have a look at him," Andy called across the lawn, and Jenifer shouted back:

"Hah!"

Cyril was already standing in the lane and when she got close to him she could see he was having some sort of struggle with himself. He kicked at the dirt and once he started toward her, then decided to wait where he was.

"Hello," she said. "Here we are again."

"Yes," he answered, "I want to tell you how sorry I am for this afternoon."

"Oh, that's all right."

"I suppose it isn't very sporting to say it, but Jenifer, I couldn't oppose my aunt; not when I live in her house, you see."

"No, perhaps you couldn't."

"She does such a lot for me, you know, and I'm not very strong and really rather a nuisance."

"Oh, Cyril." Jenifer's pique vanished when she heard the pathetic simplicity with which he stated what he believed to be a fact. She sat down on a large square stone that was one of many outlining the entrance to a drive-way and looked up at him. "Tell me," she said, "have you had any friends your own age in America? Have you ever gone to school over here?"

"No, I started in school once, just a day school, but Aunt Kate wanted to bring me to Florida, so we got Barry and he's been with us ever since. He's a nice chap and I enjoy him."

"Yes, I like him too—but there's something terribly wrong. I'm glad now that I came to tea this afternoon because I think I see what it is. You're wrapped up in cotton, Cyril. Your aunt keeps talking about you being sick and you'll never get any better if you go on this way."

"What do you think I should do?"

"Assert yourself, go out, see people."

Cyril crammed his hands in his pockets and with his head thrust forward regarded her darkly. "I told you the other day," he said, "how I feel about people. I don't want to see people."

"It's because you're afraid. Subconsciously, you're afraid to meet people."

"Jenifer, that's nonsense."

"It's true." Jenifer got up from the rock and stood very straight to face him. "You're afraid to meet people," she repeated. "And you're afraid because you think you aren't as attractive as Alfred."

"*Jenifer!*" His face was paper-white and his eyes blazed out at her. "*How dare you say such a thing!*" he shouted.

"I'm sorry." She clasped her hands behind her and stood looking at him with tears in her eyes. "Oh, Cyril," she said, "I slapped you, *hard,* just as sometimes one has to slap a person out of shock. I did it purposely."

There was a long silence while he stood away from her, and afraid of meeting each other's eyes they both stared at the ground. At last Cyril drew in his breath and let it out with a sigh. "How did you know?" he asked.

"It doesn't matter. Maybe I guessed, maybe from things you've said, but the important thing, Cyril, is this: What you believe isn't true."

He made no answer, only stood with his head bent and Jenifer touched his arm gently. "Think it over," she said, "and when I see you again. . . ."

"No, wait. Everything you told me is true," he muttered. "I am afraid to meet people; I am wrapped in cotton like a weak sick infant." He went over to the rock and sat down with his hands clenched between his knees. "I think I hate everyone in the world, Jenifer, but you."

"No you don't. You're finding out that underneath you're strong. It takes courage to face things and then decide to do something about them." Jenifer sat down on a rock beside him and began talking to him softly. The sun went down and the evening chill crept over the lane. She could hear Andy shouting for her and at last she had to stand up and say:

"I must go now. Would you like to begin asserting your independence by coming home to dinner with me?"

He looked up at her and smiled. Even in the dusk she could see that his smile was sweet and unforced. "Can you chin yourself a hundred times?" he asked.

"Of course not."

"Once?"

"Yes, once."

"I have to learn to do even that," he said. "This little excursion out into the evening air will take a lot of chinning against Aunt Kate."

"Oh, Cyril," Jenifer laughed in relief. "You're making a wonderful beginning. If you can hang onto a sense of humor everything will be fine."

"I'll hang on if you'll help me."

"You know I will."

He got up from the rock and put his hand lightly on her arm. "Jenny," he said, slipping into the name her father always used, "don't push me too fast. Be patient with me and try to remember that I'm only learning to walk."

"I'll remember."

"And you won't be angry as you were today when things go badly? For they will go badly sometimes."

"I'll never be angry again, I promise."

She laid her hand against his cheek as she did so many times with Peter and the children. It was a caress that was typically Jenifer's and her fingertips held more tenderness than she could put into words. "I'll see you tomorrow under the tree by the lake," she said, "so hurry home and start making history."

CHAPTER X

JENIFER saw Cyril every day for a week. Their hours together were short, however, for having boasted of the Jordons' good health, Jenifer noticed ruefully that the children promptly began a round of sneezing that shook the house and kept her running with fruit juices for the ones who were in bed and thinking up games for the convalescents who were shut in and bored. Rosie could read in a sing-song fashion to Bitsy and Vance, and with a radio for Susan and Neal and all the books the library could supply for the others, she managed to steal a few hours for herself. Sometimes she and Cyril sat on the boathouse deck and when they did that they had longer together but she could feel the curious eyes at the windows.

"Why don't you paint the lake?" she suggested one morning when she rushed out to go to market and found him sitting on the A. CADWALLADER bench. "Barry doesn't care when you do your lessons and it's good for you to be out here in the sunshine."

"I might." He squinted at the lake, already seeing a picture, and Jenifer went off, wondering what he would do about it. She did her marketing, laughed at Mr. Cadwallader's gruff questions about Lord Fauntleroy, and returned to find him with his easel and painting furiously, while Susan, bundled into a coat, sat solemnly beside him.

"You see, Susan," she heard him say while he squeezed paint from a tube, "when you mix yellow, like this, with blue, you make green. Have you had that in school?"

"Not yet." Susan's pigtails stuck out from under her hat

and she leaned over the palette to watch him daub the two colors together. "We just have crayons in school but I think I'll ask Jenifer to buy me some paints. Are they very expensive?"

"Um-m. I have some old ones I'll give you." Cyril went on with his painting and Jenifer turned around silently and went back to the house.

The little scene had given her an idea, so that before the next week was over Cyril had met all the children in a haphazard way and without being aware of it; all except Peter, who held himself aloof.

"Listen, Jen," Peter growled, prowling about the living room. "I won't wander out as if I'd come to pick roses and then be surprised to bump into the guy. I think he's kind of a sissy anyway."

"Oh, Peter, he isn't. He's had a terribly hard time."

"Well, so has Donny." Peter was argumentative because several facts had troubled him for some time. "Donny has too but he's never gone around crying and having complexes."

"He wasn't wounded the way Cyril was."

"Well, he was thrown clear out the back of the car. And his mother and father are just as gone as Cyril's brother and sister. It looks like a parallel case to me."

"Perhaps it is, Peter," she sighed, "but you see, Donny came here to us, to a family of normal young people. He didn't have to leave his country and learn strange ways, and he didn't have to be shut up in a house with Mrs. Van Courtlandt."

"Yeah, I see that part of it but. . . ."

"Perhaps none of us has ever known how much we've done for Donny. Perhaps he'd have been strange and twisted like Cyril if he hadn't had us. I love Donny such a lot," Jenifer said, "and at first I wanted to pet him more than the others and when I heard him crying at night I wanted to put my arms around him and cry with him, but I didn't. I'd just get a plate of cake and two glasses of milk and we'd sit on his bed and have a snack. And sometimes we'd have a snack even when he didn't cry so he wouldn't think he was being bribed."

"I never thought of doing that."

"No, but you took him fishing with you and you've let him ride Royal more than the others."

"That's 'cause he's a boy."

"So is Cyril."

"Yeah, but Donny's a swell kid." Peter picked up a china dog from the table and stood thumping it against the palm of his hand. "I don't think I could ever warm up to the guy," he grumbled.

"You never know how hot a fire can get till you light it." Jenifer went on with a letter she was writing to her father and Peter stood watching her head bent over her portfolio. He kept smacking the dog against his hand, beating out a popular song until Jenifer's pen stopped scratching and then he set the little ornament down and asked:

"Do you reckon he'd like to drive out with me to get the laundry?"

"Car or carriage?" Jenifer was reading her letter over and she asked the question idly without looking up.

"Carriage. Royal needs exercise."

"I'll ask him." She addressed an envelope, stuck on a stamp and tossed letter and envelope to Peter. "Add a postscript," she said, "and seal it while I telephone. If Cyril's aunt answers I'll guarantee he won't go. If she doesn't . . ." She went into the hall and Peter heard her say, "Hello, Barry. Peter wants to know if Cyril would like to go on an errand with him; he's driving our steed." Through the open front door she could see Lacey in the yard and she added quickly, "A friend of mine just came, Lacey Cadwallader, the girl I told you about; so why don't we all go? Can you? Fine." And then she said, lowering her voice, "Is Mrs. Van Courtlandt at home? No? Oh good, we'll come by for you.

"All set," she said blithely to Peter who was rubbing his hair and looking dismayed that his friendly gesture had collected such a crowd.

"But where will we put the basket of laundry?" he asked.

"Oh, we may not even get the laundry," Jenifer answered, gathering up her writing materials and putting them away in the desk. "We may just go for a drive." She was humming as she went off to find Lacey but she stopped to ask, "Do you want me to help you hitch up?"

Peter shook a bewildered head. "I'll be darned," he muttered to himself when he could hear Jenifer going around the house and calling Lacey, "a couple of guys can't even go off alone. How does she think I'm going to learn to know Cyril when she and Lacey'll do all the talking and this Barry bird'll horn in? It looks as if I'm just going along to drive the horse."

He plowed his hand through his wheat stubble several times while he stood in the Van Courtlandt drive and watched Jenifer place her guests in the carriage. She did give Cyril the front seat beside Peter but she squeezed in with them and sat sidewise against the iron armrest to beam on the two who were enthroned in back. When they started off Barry actually lounged, as nearly as one could lounge on the hard narrow seat, and the original idea of Peter becoming acquainted with Cyril was lost in the ease with which Barry was learning to know Lacey.

The late February day was warm and the carriage fanned a little breeze as it jolted over the sandy back roads, so that the fringe on its top waved gaily. Royal stepped along, his ears flicking back at the clucks that Peter, for lack of something better to do, kept sending him, or cocked to listen for bird-songs or a sudden noise that might give him a chance to shy. Peter held the lines laced through his fingers, his hands correctly vertical, and wished he could think of something to say.

He and Cyril rode in silence listening to Lacey and Barry compare notes on their college days while Jenifer hung over the back of the seat. He had no idea what the other boy's thoughts were and was becoming most uncomfortable when Cyril turned to him and suddenly burst out:

"I say, you do drive well."

There was admiration in his voice and Peter answered modestly, "Oh, Royal's easy to drive. I think having been ridden makes him sensitive to the least touch on his bit. Want to drive him?"

"I'd like to, sometime."

"Shall we change places?"

"Not now, thanks, I'd much rather watch the way you do it. What sort of bit do you use?"

"A snaffle, the same one I ride him with." Peter was on familiar ground now and he shifted his lines to one hand while he demonstrated how easily Royal handled. Cyril leaned a little forward to watch and they forgot the others until Lacey cried:

"Oh, Peter, stop, so we can pick some wild flowers. Those clumps of red things are gorgeous and I want some for school tomorrow."

So he pulled up and he and Cyril inspected Royal's harness and looked at his feet and talked horseshoeing while the others walked along the road picking small red and yellow blossoms.

Barry tried to pick. He managed to gather a stalk or two, but he was too busy looking at Lacey.

"Goodness, he's blossoming out himself," Jenifer thought, watching him hand Lacey a sprig and look at it as if he wished it could turn into an orchid. Lacey was sitting on the ground arranging her bouquet and Barry was bending over to help her. Behind them was an orange grove, its trees filled with golden-ripe fruit, the air around it rich with the scent of oranges that had fallen and broken. "I wish we didn't have to break this up," Jenifer said reluctantly. "Has anyone a watch?"

No one had but Barry, and his had stopped, so she squinted at the sun that was much too low and suggested to Peter, "Don't you think we should go? You have to feed Royal and put him to bed before retreat."

"I guess so, but I've got my trusty orderly to help me," Peter laughed as they got back into the carriage.

"Which one is that?" Cyril asked, and Jenifer shook her head.

"If you knew us better," she sighed, "you wouldn't have to ask. It's poor Alice."

As soon as Royal got the carriage turned around and found he was headed for home he really extended his trot.

"I'll breeze him," Peter shouted. "Hold on."

They racketed along until they came to the asphalt where Peter slowed to a walk. "Gosh," Cyril said, in a quaint mixture of American-British slang, "that was tops."

Royal's sides were working like bellows when they drove up to the stable doors and when Peter jumped over the wheel and began unfastening the harness Cyril followed him to help loosen the straps.

"I'll have to walk him to cool him," Peter said, with a worried frown for Royal, who was blowing and shaking his head. "Want to go down the lane and back with me?"

The two boys started off with a disappointed horse tagging along behind them, and Lacey and Barry were still in the carriage picking up scattered stalks of flowers from the seat when Jenifer, climbing down, saw Andy in the kitchen door. "Hi," she called, "it's too bad you have to work for a living or you could have gone with us."

Andy's lip was out as far as his jaw but as it often stuck out when he teased, she introduced him to Barry and had to look into his eyes to see that he was hurt.

"Miss Cadwallader," he said, stepping close to the carriage and holding out his hand to help Lacey down, "have you forgotten you invited me to dine? I went to your house and no one was at home."

Lacey leaned out from under the fringe to laugh at him. "People don't dine at five o'clock," she reminded.

"No, but I was invited for six."

"It isn't *six!*" Jenifer cried in dismay.

"It's ten minutes after and we have already had retreat, such few of us as gathered, and the flag has been put to bed."

"Oh, my!" Lacey barely touched Andy's hand or the step as she sprang down. She was watching Barry who landed behind her looking as if he would like to snatch his pupil and run up the lane.

"Will there be trouble?" she asked, lifting her eyebrows.

"I'm afraid so. Mrs. Van Courtlandt went to a bridge party and I only hope we can get in before she does. I'll have to hurry." He held out his hand to Andy and said quickly to Lacey, "I'll call for you tomorrow night at eight. Is that all right?"

Lacey nodded and he said, "Thanks, Jenifer," and went rushing off.

"Why is he calling for you at eight?" Andy demanded, glaring at the road where Barry was whistling and waving his arms. "Have you got a date with him?"

"He asked me to go to the movies."

"You have a date with me."

"I hadn't heard of it."

"Well then, we have a court martial on."

"There isn't one scheduled."

Lacey's head was going higher and higher and Andy was matching it horizontally with his chin and his lip. "You'll be confined to quarters for this stunt you pulled today," he threatened. "You'll have to do k.p."

"Then I'll hurry so I can be through by eight o'clock."

He looked around to see what had become of Jenifer and when she was nowhere in sight he leaned against the carriage and asked anxiously, "For the second time, will you marry me?"

"For the second time," Lacey answered with spirit, "why should I?"

"Why, because . . . because I can help you with the k.p. and can take you to the movies every night."

"For the second time—no." Lacey slipped under his arm and with a little laugh disappeared as quickly and completely as Jenifer had done.

CHAPTER XI

KATHERINE VAN COURTLANDT was the kind of woman who walked in her garden in the crisp morning air and audited her emotions. She ran her life on a paying basis and when an asset turned into a liability she immediately did something about it. Just now Cyril was upsetting the even tenor of her days by rushing off down the lane at every opportunity and, although she hated to admit it even to herself, by being openly defiant.

She looked through a towering screen of poinsettias at smoke curling from the low white house in the lane and wondered what there was about Jenifer Jordon that drew Cyril to her, as unresisting as a nail to a magnet. To wonder was to act, and like old King Cole who had only to call for things, she called for her chauffeur and her car.

Mrs. Van Courtlandt never had to rush in and dress to go anywhere. She always happened to be wearing just the correct outfit for whatever expedition she wished to embark upon, so, quite smart in a gray suit and a fur scarf of six little minks nipped to each other's tails, she seated herself in her car and traversed the few hundred yards along the lane. A dull-witted servant girl answered her imperious ring of the Jordon doorbell and informed her that Jenifer had gone to do the marketing. Then Mrs. Van Courtlandt, who had rarely bought so much as a cake of soap for herself, set out on Jenifer's trail to Mr. Cadwallader's.

It was a gray morning and Jenifer, unlike Katherine Van Courtlandt, had to get for herself whatever she wanted. When she had opened her eyes she had wished wearily that reveille wouldn't go off so early, that Rosie could shorten the grocery list, that the children could remember what they did with their belongings, even that Cyril wouldn't be hunting her up expecting her to be bright and cheery. She didn't feel bright and cheery. She ached all over and she was tired.

Sitting up in bed, rubbing her legs, she thought the outside of her felt all right; it was only the inside of her bones that was tired. And her voice. Very often lately her voice was too tired to talk. It came out with a breathless distant sound and was apt to leave a sentence unfinished. For several days she had urged Cyril to paint Gwenn, so she could lie on the boathouse deck and pretend to nap. Gwenn twinkled and posed but after a little of it Cyril would throw down his brush to come sit beside her.

"Let's talk, Jenny," he would say. "A day is wasted when I don't talk with you."

So Jenifer would manage to prop herself against the rail, liking the way his eyes were gathering new lights in them and noticing that his mouth was sweet now and had a quick upward quirk at its ends.

But today . . . today, dragging herself wearily out of bed, she wished Gwenn would come home pouting prettily to have her portrait finished and all the smaller children could be kept in school until midnight.

So Mrs. Van Courtlandt, knowing nothing of this, walked into the dim corner grocery for a chance meeting with the girl who was undermining the good qualities of her nephew and encountered a strange scene.

Mr. Cadwallader was running with a glass of water and he pushed past her without even seeing her while the Jordon girl, of all queer places to be, was stretched full-length on the counter.

"Here, Jenifer," he was shouting, "drink this and lie still. Dang it, I said lie still!"

"But I feel all right now, Mr. Cadwallader. Just for a minute I was. . . ."

"Just for a minute you were flat on the floor."

She tried to sit up but he pushed her back and ran his hand awkwardly over her hair. "Your forehead's as wet as a dishmop," he scolded. "A fine thing, you wearing yourself out for a parcel of kids. And as for that earl or duke or whatever he is, I wish he'd go back home where he belongs." Mrs. Van Courtlandt made a small noise behind him and he turned to look at her. "Sorry, ma'am," he said, "I'll wait on you as soon's I can, but this girl's sick. There's a chair over there if you want to sit down."

"Could I help you?"

Jenifer had closed her eyes because she felt better with them shut, but at the sound of Katherine Van Courtlandt's voice they flew open again. "Oh!" she gasped, hoping Mr. Cadwallader would talk less freely before a stranger; but he was launched on a subject that had worried him, and as he didn't know when he would ever again have Jenifer in a position where she had to listen to him, he went on relentlessly:

"No thanks. This girl's got to rest. Always doing for somebody, that's her trouble. Thinks she's Atlas and can carry the world on her shoulders. Dang it, it's my private opinion that her father ought to come home and let the war take care of itself." He was stroking Jenifer's hair gently and she wanted to reach up and clasp his horny old hand. She felt stronger now but knew if she moved they would have a scene, so she lay still on the hard boards and listened to his voice.

"Oh, I know the General thought he had things fixed," he was explaining to his unknown audience, "but the housekeeper left and there's just Jenifer and that dumb Rosie to run things. Gave up her school, gave up all her good times, gave up everything, to take care of eight children. Could you do it? Could I?" He offered the astounded woman who was staring at him no chance to speak but answered for them both, "You're danged right, we couldn't. And now that nutty boy comes along, all full of complexes."

At that Jenifer did sit up. The cans on the shelves swayed crazily but she held onto the edges of the counter. "Mr. Cadwallader," she managed to say, "this is Cyril's aunt."

"It is? Well, I've been wantin' to know her." He took off his glasses and stared as very few people had ever openly stared at Katherine Van Courtlandt. "Howdy, ma'am," he said, holding Jenifer in the crook of his arm, "you're a very lucky woman that this girl here took your boy in hand before you plum ruined him."

"Do you think so?" Her tone was icy but it failed to chill him.

"Think so? Dang it, I know so. He's a nice boy and Jenifer's got him so's he'll come in my store now and act like any of the other high-school kids that come in. I've been watchin' the change in him and I've been seein' Jenifer gettin' pale and peaked from it. She's wore out, what with his ructions and the children's ructions, and I aim to see she doesn't have any more of it."

"Oh, please." Jenifer eased her legs over the edge of the counter and would have slid to the floor but his arm still held her.

"You are quite right," Mrs. Van Courtlandt said with an emphatic nod, "she is definitely undertaking too much."

She looked at the pale girl in the protecting circle of the old man's arm, noticing that even with her hair tumbled and wet from the unsteady handling of a glass of water, she was very lovely.

Jenifer looked thin under her baggy sweater and to a woman who had a massage or a facial or a pine-scented bath when she was weary, she looked pathetic and young. "I'll drive her home," she said briskly, "and see that she's put to bed."

"I'm takin' her home myself." Mr. Cadwallader stated the fact flatly and put his glasses back on. "You sit right there, Jenifer, until I find my sign." He released her shoulders to go into his office for the "STORE CLOSED" card he hung on the door when he wanted to go fishing, and Jenifer promptly put her feet on the floor.

"He's making a terrible fuss, Mrs. Van Courtlandt," she said, smiling and standing up straight to prove nothing was wrong, "so please don't mind what he said about Cyril. Cyril had nothing to do with my fainting this morning."

"I wonder. Cyril's temperament can be very exhausting."

Jenifer leaned against the counter and tried to smooth back her hair. Things were muddled inside her head but she knew enough of Cyril's aunt to understand that whatever view she had of Cyril was a stamped photograph on her mind. Her mind had a whole album of such poses and Jenifer saw no use in arguing about it. In fact, she saw no use in anything but getting home where she belonged.

"And so, my dear," Mrs. Van Courtlandt was saying, as if she had been talking steadily and Jenifer had missed it, "I'm going to see that you're tucked into bed and then I'm going to send over one of my maids to take care of you. I can't let you suffer for what you have done for Cyril."

"Oh please. . . ." Jenifer lifted her head to answer proudly, and then to her great surprise, she began to cry. She turned her back and bent over the counter as her sobs shook her and Mr. Cadwallader came running.

"Now see what you've done!" he shouted, slamming his hat on the floor. "Messin' in, you and your boy. There now," he soothed, "we'll get Lacey home from school and everything'll be all right. Come on, honey, the car's out back."

He tried to turn her away from the counter, but Mrs. Van Courtlandt had come forward. "No, wait," she urged, suddenly very human and a little frightened. "Between us, we're only upsetting her more. Suppose you sit down, my dear, and rest for a moment while Mr. Cadwallader and I straighten things out."

But Jenifer only shook her head. "I'm all right now," she said, wiping her eyes. "I don't know what's making me act this way. I don't know when I've ever cried and been so stupid before."

"It's because you're overtired and worried. Everyone does it sometimes." Katherine Van Courtlandt's voice could be very persuasive, and before she knew it, Jenifer found herself leaning back in the limousine, with Mr. Cadwallader looking anxiously in the window and asking over and over:

"You're sure you don't want me to go with you, Jenifer? You're sure now?"

"I'm sure," she smiled. "I'm fine now, really."

"I'll be over before supper and I'll telephone Rosie you're comin'."

He stepped back as the car rolled away and Jenifer leaned forward to wave to him. "Dear Mr. Cadwallader," she said, swallowing a lump in her throat, "he's been so good to us."

Mrs. Van Courtlandt was very efficient when she arrived home with Jenifer. She was surprised to find the Jordon house so attractive and thought it no wonder the girl had given out. She herself, she decided, would be dead. She established Jenifer on a divan in the living room and seeing no bell to ring, went off to hunt Rosie. "Bring a glass of milk," she ordered, finding Rosie in her hat and coat and crying excitedly:

"Is Miss Jenifer sick? I was on my way to the store for her because I couldn't understand a word Mr. Cadwallader said."

"She's all right, but resting. Just bring the milk." She was suddenly aware of weeping on the lawn and went to the door as Bitsy, followed by Rollo, climbed the back steps.

"I hurt my finger," Bitsy wailed, "and I want Jenifer to fix it. It needs 'hesive tape and I can't find Jenifer."

"I'll bandage it for you," Katherine Van Courtlandt surprised herself by saying. "I'm Cyril's aunt and I'll bandage your finger."

When she finally got back to the living room with the glass of milk she found Jenifer fast asleep. She lay with her arms flung above her head, in the complete abandonment of a child, and not even the joyful licks Rollo gave her could wake her. She only sighed and turned her cheek into the pillow and, with a look of distaste, Mrs. Van Courtlandt scooped up Rollo and carried him out.

This was the sort of situation in which she excelled, and in a few moments she had her chauffeur speeding across town for her own housekeeper's sister. Bitsy went with him, and Vance, whom the kindergarten teacher had dropped off at the gate; and when they were gone she started Rosie, awed and submissive, on the lunch.

Jenifer still slept and it was when she sat down beside her, wondering what to do next, that she saw Cyril through the window. He was running across the lawn and she jumped up to meet him at the door.

"Aunt Kate," he shouted, "what's wrong? Paul stopped by with the car and he had Bitsy and Vance with him."

"There is nothing wrong, Cyril." Mrs. Van Courtlandt spoke positively and from force of habit he almost believed her. "Jenifer is tired."

"But why is she tired? She wasn't tired yesterday."

"It was yesterday that made her tired, and the day before that, and I suppose a great many days." She closed the front door behind her and stood looking at Cyril on the bottom step. "Her friend who owns the store says you have added a great burden to Jenifer."

"Oh, Aunt Kate, *no!*"

"He says so. It seems the villagers have discussed us quite freely and, I must say, it is a unique experience to find that our family can be a burden to anyone. I intend to rectify it immediately."

"Aunt Kate! Do you know what you're saying?"

"Perfectly." She walked down the steps and stood looking thoughtfully into the distance. "You're in no way responsible for Jenifer's leaving school," she said at last, "but with Ellin coming to take charge she can have lessons with you and Barry. And as soon as she is able I shall give a party for her." She felt his silence behind her and turned to say quickly, "Whether you like it or not I shall entertain for her. If she needs gaiety I shall see that she has it."

"Aunt Kate, I'll tell her why."

"I don't think you will, Cyril," she returned coldly, "you've told her quite enough already."

He sat down on the step and dropped his head in his hands. "Is it because you've discovered how wonderful she is that you want to do these things?" he looked up to ask. "Have you got fond of her?"

"That has nothing to do with it. She's a very pretty girl

but it's a matter of repaying her for what everyone seems to think she has done for you."

"She's done everything for me, if that's what you mean. I didn't care to live until I found Jenifer . . . and now I can't bear to think of what life will be without her."

He made the statement so simply that his aunt looked down at him with an expression of pity. Then she saw the car turn in and walked across the grass to talk with the woman who was sitting on the back seat, holding Bitsy on her lap.

"I'm glad you could come, Ellin," she said, opening the door and lifting Bitsy out. "Did you bring a bag with you?"

"Thank ye, ma'am. Yis, I have enough for a few days and me brother will fetch me more."

Ellin McCarthy got out of the car and leaned over to shake the wrinkles out of her ample black skirt. She was a big jolly woman with twinkling eyes above a button nose and her Irish brogue rolled out musically. " 'Tis a pleasure to do what I can for ye, after ye bein' so good to me Patrick," she said, "and I'm glad to be takin' the motherless darlin's under me wing."

Cyril sat on the step and watched Paul take Ellin's bag from the car, watched Bitsy pull Ellin around the house. He knew there was nothing he could say to Jenifer. She had no knowledge of people who helped others without love or kindliness. He was ashamed, but there was nothing he could do unless he hurt her. Then she could have the satisfaction of sending his aunt home and of dismissing Ellin—and how much better off would she be? Cyril sighed and watched the afternoon slide away and wished Jenifer would wake.

She did at last, when the children were home from school and tiptoeing in and out, when Rosie had been moved into the girls' barracks and Ellin was settled in and teaching Susan to sew.

"Well," Jenifer said, sitting up and stretching, "I must have had quite a nap." She smiled at Cyril who was keeping his vigil in a chair across the room and added, "Yet I seem to remember so many things. Is there somebody strange in the kitchen?"

"It's Ellin McCarthy," he told her. "Aunt Kate brought her over and she's going to stay with you."

"Oh, how divine! I know I should go out to speak to her but . . ." She flopped back among the pillows. "It seems such an effort." She turned her head so she could look out the window and Cyril came to sit beside her. "Cyril," she asked, so low he leaned forward to hear, "have I failed?"

"Failed? Good heavens, no, Jenny."

"I was going to do so much," she said slowly. "I told Daddy I would. And when Mrs. Sanders left I was so sure I could manage. And now look at me, flat as a pancake." She tried to laugh but it was a feeble effort and Cyril dropped down on the floor beside her.

"Jenifer, don't talk about failing," he begged. "Everyone has to have help, from the President and General Eisenhower down."

"But I had help. I had Rosie and Peter and Lacey and Andy; and the children all tried to help." She closed her eyes and sighed. "I do so hate people who fail."

"Well, you haven't failed. If you're ever tempted to think so, take a good look at me. If anyone ever had a living monument to her success . . ." Cyril had tried to be light in his banter but he dropped pretense and lifted her hand from the afghan to lay it against his cheek. "Oh, Jenny, Jenny," he whispered, "you're wonderful. Don't ever doubt it and don't ever, ever let anyone make you believe anything else."

CHAPTER XII

"I'M TAKING my place in the world," Jenifer announced, sitting at her dressing table and looking into the mirror at Peter who lounged on the bed behind her. "I'm having a dance given for me and I have a new dress for it and you can open the closet door and look at it if you like." She held a pink camellia on each side of her head and leaned forward to study the effect. "Like it?" she asked.

"It looks okay." Peter answered without really seeing the flowers. "Do I have to go?"

"Of course you do. Mrs. Van Courtlandt—I mean Aunt Kate—wouldn't like it if you don't show up."

"Huh? Since when did you start calling her Aunt Kate?"

"Since yesterday morning. She asked us to and I said we'd try to remember." Jenifer held both flowers above one ear and regarded them intently. "I'll tell you a secret," she said. "She's beginning to like me better."

"Didn't she always like you?"

"Humhum." Jenifer shook her head and one of the camellias bounced off. "She didn't like me at all," she said, reaching down to the floor for the flower. "She pretended she did but her eyes had steel splinters in them. She didn't like any of us."

"Well, jumpin' monkeys! Why did you keep on going over there?"

"Because she wanted me to. She liked to have me study with Cyril and have Paul do Ellin's marketing, and give a party for Cyril and me. She was easing her conscience."

"What for?"

"Oh, because Mr. Cadwallader, bless his dear soul, made her feel like a heel. It's all pretty complicated but I figured it out." Jenifer began brushing her hair back from her face and Peter got up from the bed.

"I don't get it," he said.

She started over with the flowers but slid around on the dressing-table bench to beg, "You *will* go to the party, won't you? Mrs. Van Courtlandt, Aunt Kate I mean, let you invite Paul Seton so you'd have someone to talk to."

"Where's she going to find any men?"

"Andy's bringing some officers for the older crowd and Barry knows some professors at Rollins and some of her friends have boys in school out there. Now don't ask me why they're in college in wartime," she said hastily, "they're just there, that's all. Are you coming?"

"Aw, I guess so."

"Then hurry and dress. And did you see the pink roses and lilies of the valley in the refrigerator? They're made into a sort of bouquet to hold in my hand, from Cyril. But my dearest beloved sent the camellias."

"Who's he?"

"Mr. Cadwallader. All in a box, and everything. Now hurry."

Jenifer, as she told Peter, had been well aware of Katherine Van Courtlandt's feeling toward the Jordons. At first she had been too weak to mind, and later the eagerness with which Cyril welcomed her into his home and the joy he showed in running freely in and out of hers meant more to her than his aunt's coldness. Mrs. Van

Courtlandt delighted in heaping favors upon Jenifer, in being Lady Bountiful with a magic wand, and for Cyril's sake she accepted all this. On the surface everything was serene and there had been only one clash, and that had been about the dance and had come from Andy.

"Whose date are you?" he had demanded of Lacey, "Barry's, or mine?"

"If it's going to cause such a commotion," Lacey had answered sweetly, "I can go alone. Or one of you can take me and one can bring me home."

"Not by a hatful." Andy had been stamping around the Cadwallader living room and now he threw a magazine on a table and shouted, "All right, if that's the way you want it, we'll go like we've been going for the last three weeks—as the three Ys; Lacey, Barry, and Andy."

"We will not." Lacey leaned back in her chair and laughed at him. "I'll go with you, you big silly."

"You will?"

"Of course I will. I'd planned to."

"Then why didn't you *say* so!"

"Because you hadn't asked me. I can't say 'Andy, I'd like to have you take me to the dance.' Ladies don't do that."

"Listen." Andy planted his feet wide apart and stared down at her. "I ask you something every time I see you. I'm always asking you one question. . . ."

"And the answer is, no." Lacey got up and pushed him into the hall. "Don't say you want to marry me because we look so pretty dancing together. I don't doubt we do look pretty but let's try it awhile longer."

She had told Jenifer about it when they were out in Lacey's car and they had laughed together until jenifer asked seriously, "Don't you want to marry Andy, Lacey?"

"That hasn't anything to do with it." Lacey was suddenly sober. She eased the car into a parking space before a store and pulled on the brake. "Andy," she began, "hasn't said . . ." And then Barry, who was waiting for them, poked his head in the window and the sentence was left unfinished.

Jenifer wondered about it while she was dressing for her party. Something was troubling Lacey for even though she teased Andy she often looked at him with a sweet tenderness in her blue eyes. And Jenifer wondered if he had noticed it.

She sat on the side of her bed in her flowered cotton house coat and her gold sandals. The sandals were new and never had she parted with a shoe-ration coupon so willingly. She held her feet out to admire them and after several minutes of infinite satisfaction looked up at her dress. It hung on the closet door, a pale pink froth of net, as delectable as strawberry mousse.

"Get a pink dress," Cyril had whispered when she and his aunt had started to town. "Lolly always had a pink dress. She said it made her feel gay."

They were standing in the hall waiting for Mrs. Van Courtlandt to give the housekeeper her orders for the day and Jenifer had whispered back, "Your aunt says white."

"Buy pink if you can."

So Jenifer bought pink, adoring the dress but figuring carefully in her checkbook and sighing a little over the drop it made in her balance. The dress hung now like a pale-pink dream on the closet door and she got up and was caressing it when Ellin came in.

"Darlin', did ye think I wasn't comin' to hilp ye?" Ellin cried, puffing a little and smiling. "The spalpeens would have it that I teach thim an Irish jig and me jiggin' days are gone foriver. But we've plinty of time and Rosie is bringin' your supper."

She bustled about the room and Jenifer said, "Really, Ellin, I can manage alone and I'm not a bit hungry. Gwenn will straighten up after me."

"Gwenn is havin' a fit that she isn't invited. 'Only one year younger than Peter I am,' says she, stampin' her foot, 'and he's going.'" Ellin was putting Jenifer's bedroom slippers in the closet and she laughed comfortably. "We'll have our hands full with Miss Gwenn one of these days," she prophesied, "and her not nearly so sweet and pretty as Alice."

She came out of the closet as Rosie stopped in the door with a tray. "Now eat your supper," she ordered, shooing Rosie out and setting the tray on the desk. "We'll have no more faintin' tonight. And while ye're doin' it I'll see if me boy has his shoes shined."

She whisked out and Jenifer ate a little and waited for her to come back. Always before, when she dressed to go out, the children had clustered around her, getting into her things and hindering more than they helped. It seemed strange to be sitting quietly in her own room with only Bitsy's bed in the corner to show it wasn't entirely hers. She knew now how other girls must feel in their privacy and while she enjoyed it she was a little lonely and was glad when Ellin came back.

The pink dress was slipped over her head without mussing her curls or disturbing the camellias above each ear and she lifted her arms while Ellin fastened it. "Ellin," she said, looking into the mirror, "I don't see how life could change so in ten days. All the good times and . . . you're almost like having a mother again."

"And it's what ye deserve." Ellin clicked her tongue against her cheek. "Whoiver heard of a young girl makin' an old woman of hersilf! There, now ye're ready and ye can show yirself to the audience that's waitin' in the livin' room."

Jenifer had never seen the children so awed. When she came through the door they stared at her respectfully and stood in a circle around her while she turned like a mannequin for them.

"Oh Jenifer, you're just beautiful," Susan breathed, clasping her fat hands under her chin, "just like Snow White, only you're pink. Isn't she, Neal?"

"Umhum." Neal nodded solemnly and sat down on the floor beside Donny who was looking up at Jenifer as if seeing an angel.

"Do you like my dress, Donny?" she asked.

"Yes," he answered slowly, barely moving his lips, his gaze enraptured, "Mamma had one like it once."

"Oh darling." Jenifer would have dropped down beside him had not Alice pushed out two unusually clean hands to stop her. "Please be careful, Jenifer," she begged. "It'll wrinkle. Donny just likes to look at you. He feels all right about it, don't you, Donny?"

"Sure." Lights came back into his eyes and he grinned but Jenifer did stoop to kiss the top of his head.

"Play checkers with him," she said to Gwenn who stood with her hands behind her, her head tilted appraisingly. Gwenn approved of Jenifer's dress although she wished she were wearing it herself and was about to say so when Peter came in.

He wore his best gray slacks with a tan-plaid sports jacket and looked uncomfortably neat and almost handsome. Jenifer wished she dared suggest a change to the coat that matched his trousers but the fact that he was dressed at all was such a triumph she was afraid to risk it.

"Well, let's go," he growled, "and get it over."

Vance ran for the flowers in the refrigerator, and since an early April evening is cool in Florida Jenifer threw her polo coat around her shoulders.

"You ought to have a white fur bunny jacket," Gwenn criticized with a frown. "I wouldn't think of going without one."

"Then I wouldn't think of going at all," Jenifer laughed. "Nobody will see my coat anyway because we'll be early." She started to follow Peter and then from force of habit turned to say, "Bitsy, go straight to bed; Susan, see that Neal does his lessons."

"Now, what do ye think I'm here for?" Ellin stopped her. "Ye're goin' off to have a good time and if there's anything here be done, I'll do it. We'll settle down, so run on with ye. And remimber," she said from the front door watching Jenifer run down the steps, "as I always said to me own children, 'pretty is as pretty does.'"

Jenifer laughed again and thought it was lovely not to have to worry about how things were going at home. She almost skipped as she picked her way along the lane and by the time she and Peter reached the Van Courtlandts' her heart was pounding with excitement and she had forgotten the children completely.

The house was softly lighted and except for the grand piano the long drawing room had been cleared for dancing. There had been the problem of music in wartime, the kind of music young people like to dance to, until Andy had asked permission of his commanding officer to bring in five young soldiers who played in the post band.

"It's not exactly according to army regulations," he told Mrs. Van Courtlandt, "but the boys are all out of big orchestras, and they're so crazy about playing together that if you'd like to invite them to the party I think they'd rather toot than dance."

"Do you mean not pay them?"

Andy nodded and she lifted her eyebrows in surprise. "Perhaps I could give them each a War Bond," she suggested. "You know, the government urges people to buy War Bonds."

She looked up so innocently that he had to grin even though he said positively, "No. A lot of us are in the army now and if we were allowed to earn money on the side Uncle Sam would have nothing but a bunch of tired soldiers. No, they're just guests."

So now the five young soldiers were standing in the empty room with Andy and Barry and, odd as it seemed, they had come to a party carrying a saxophone, a cornet, an accordion, and a set of drums. Peter promptly attached himself to them and that was the end of him for the evening.

When other guests began to arrive Jenifer stood with Cyril beside Mrs. Van Courtlandt, and smiled at the way she was introduced to people whom she had known for a year. The high school girls said hello to her and smiled with interest on Cyril, and young officers gave him a nod but forgot to let go of her hand.

"So nice to see you," Mrs. Van Courtlandt would murmur, even when Jenifer made the introductions. "Have you met my nephew? And of course you know Miss Jordon, *General* Jordon's daughter, who is rapidly becoming my niece by adoption."

Jenifer thought it was almost as if her father were present. He figured so prominently in the introductions that had his hearty voice boomed out she would have felt no surprise. She was enjoying it but every now and then she glanced anxiously at Cyril to see how he was bearing up. He was very correct in a dinner jacket but his mouth looked set and she knew it was because of the uniforms that kept pouring in. So she was glad when the ordeal was over, when she could stop clutching her flowers, could lay them on a chair and dance with him. The five soldiers had drifted toward the piano and were playing. Their music was rhythmic and continuous, although often during the evening first one and then another would lay down his instrument as Barry had told him to do and go off to dance with a girl he knew.

"Isn't it fun, Cyril?" Jenifer said, matching her steps to his and loving the way her skirt swirled out around her.

"It's tops. You aren't tired?" He held her away to look at her and she laughed happily.

"I feel wonderful!" she answered as a young second lieutenant tapped Cyril on the shoulder. "I feel . . ." She went dancing off with the young lieutenant and after that she turned from one pair of arms to another.

Cyril danced dutifully with other girls but his dark eyes followed her. She was a new Jenifer, gay and beautiful, and he wondered if he would ever again find the girl he had known. The idea of Jenifer being lost to him forever tormented him until he had to tell her.

"You aren't Jenifer," he said, when they were sitting on the stairs together eating a late supper. "You're lovely— but you aren't Jenifer."

"I am, underneath." She lifted a forkful of creamed chicken and nodded above it, "You'll see. Tomorrow I'll be just Jenifer again."

"I wonder. Your telephone will ring constantly from now on, you'll go on dates and to post dances. . . ."

"I'm not going to dances," she scoffed. "At my age? Don't be silly."

"I think Aunt Kate hopes you will."

"Then Aunt Kate can just go on hoping." Jenifer ate a few bites before she said seriously, "There may be some high school boys around, Cyril, there often are, with Peter, but I won't be having dates."

"You're sure, Jenny?" He reached out to touch her hand as she set her plate on the step and she looked up to smile at him.

"Of course, I'm sure," she said. "I wouldn't give up our lessons together, and our walks, and the fun we have after dinner for all the dates in the world. Please don't worry about it, for if you do I'll wish your aunt hadn't given the party."

"I won't. But Jenny, we'll be leaving the first of May and think of the weeks I've wasted in being such a moron."

"You've been sweet—and very intriguing. I might not have noticed you if you hadn't been so moody and odd." Jenifer wrinkled up her nose at him and waved to Andy who was going through the hall with two plates of ice cream. "Where's Lacey?" she called.

"Looking like a quarterback calling signals in the middle of a football huddle," he answered. "Do you kids want this ice cream? I can't get near her."

"Bring it up."

They held out their hands and Andy sat on the step below them. In a few minutes a crowd had gathered and Jenifer swept her skirts aside for a boy to sit above her and was talking with another one through the banisters.

"You know, Cyril," Andy said, watching her, "I don't think you and I are so good at parties. Maybe we're more the domestic type, huh?"

"We probably are."

"Then I guess I'd better go and find Lacey. I don't suppose she's missed me," he sighed, getting up, "but there's something I want to ask her."

Jenifer broke off her conversation through the banisters and turned to say teasingly, "What reason will you give her this time, Andy?"

"I don't know." He tucked in his crooked lip and squared his shoulders. "Something will come to me," he decided, blinking thoughtfully. "It always has."

CHAPTER XIII

JENIFER was lying in the hammock that was stretched between two live oak trees on the back lawn. Sometimes she watched Peter and Donny who were washing the carriage by the stable door; sometimes she turned her head to be sure Neal was keeping out from under Royal's hoofs while he grazed him; now and then she sat up to look at Lacey and Andy who were in the rowboat fishing; or hung precariously over the hammock's edge to see what Cyril was painting.

"Aren't we the luckiest family?" she said, lying back and pillowing her head in her arms. "Ellin's baking a cake and Rosie's icing it and Bitsy and Vance are contentedly licking the bowl. I can't imagine me with nothing on my mind but to think about what a good time I had last night."

"We did have fun." Cyril stepped back to squint at his canvas and Jenifer cried:

"Fun! Don't be so sparing in your praise, Mr. Carlington. It was divine, but divine! I wonder what Andy and Lacey are doing out there." She bounced up again and had she but known it they were having an argument. Lacey was whipping her line around and Andy had stopped rowing to scold her.

"Look," he said, "you're supposed to *catch* a fish, not knock him out."

"Well, this old reel's no good."

The line went zing again and Andy ducked. "Uncle Sam isn't going to like it if you put out my eye," he yelled.

"Then take your eye back to the post where it's safe."

The boat was drifting to shore and Andy gave a tug at the oars. "You aren't much of a fisherman, are you?" he grinned, watching her hook catch on the dock.

"I'm a good fisherman." Lacey jerked her rod, then swayed it back and forth until the hook came free. "If you'd taken me over by the water lilies as I asked you to. . . ."

"You'd have caught the duck that couldn't fly North with the others."

"Pooh." She reeled in her line and threw the rod in the bottom of the boat. "I can't do anything when you keep making cracks," she wailed. "You get me so *confused*."

"Then how about letting me take over the family fishing, for life? I could catch enough fish to support us."

"Andy," Lacey watched him move the boat along with strong swift strokes, "you keep giving me the most ridiculous reason why I should marry you. Don't you ever get tired of it?"

"What if I do?" he shrugged. "If I stop promoting myself you'll forget me, but if I can think up enough reasons. . . ."

"But none of them are any good. They're just—reasons."

"And you won't marry me?"

Lacey shook her head and trailed her fingers in the water watching the ripples they made. "No."

"Okay, then as you say, I'd better stop making a fool of myself." He let the boat drift and sat hunched over the oars, his red head bent. "I've given every argument I know," he muttered, "and clowned and played the fool;

yet I can't bear to give you up. I just love you so much."

"*Andy!*" Lacey jerked her hand out of the water and sat up. "What did you say?" she cried.

"I said I just love you so much."

"Oh, *Andy!*" The boat rocked as she held out her arms and shouted, "The answer is *yes!* Yes, Andy, yes!"

It was a second or two before he could believe what he had heard, before he could make a lunge for her. Then the oars got in his way, the minnow bucket upset, he tripped over the rod, so that he sprawled at her feet clutching her knees. The boat rocked from one side to the other and Lacey grabbed him around the neck from fright as much as from love.

"Well, blow me down, am I dumb," he panted. "You don't mean you'll *marry* me!"

He was trying to balance the boat and she released him a little knowing he would tow her to shore if they went over. "Of course I will, Andy," she said. "I would have a long time ago if you had said you loved me."

"But you knew I did!"

He reached up to put his arms around her then let out a howl of pain. "Get that darned fish hook out of my leg!" he yelled.

"Oh dear." Lacey looked over his shoulder at what little of the rod she could see, then eased herself around him and sat down among the flopping minnows in the bottom of the boat. "Andy," she groaned, gritting her teeth while she peeked under the cuff of his trousers, "it's caught in you, what shall I do?"

"Keep me for life I guess, you can't throw me back."

He wriggled around until he could take his knife from his pocket and it was at that moment that Jenifer sat up again.

"What under the sun are they doing," she wondered aloud, "with Andy lying in the bottom of the boat?" And then unable to satisfy her curiosity without a pair of field glasses, she called, "Donny, go tell them it's time for retreat."

Donny dropped his sponge and went running down the slope. "Yoo-hoo," he shouted, standing on the dock and waving his arms, "we're ready for retreat. Hey, *retreat!*"

"We'll take it out here," Andy sat up to answer, wincing when Lacey cut the hook from the line. "Tell 'em to go ahead."

"Can you make it, darling?" Lacey asked, wringing her hands and looking at the hook as if she could wish it out of Andy's shin.

"If you'll roll up my pants leg and help me up I could make it standing on my head."

So when the notes of Peter's saxophone called the others to form a line on the lawn, Lacey and Andy watched the flag come down like two shipwrecked mariners clinging together.

"My goodness, what's happened?" Jenifer called, standing on the dock and watching Lacey row in.

"He's caught a fish hook in his leg," Lacey answered, "the poor lamb." She was very important about throwing the tow rope to Jenifer, about helping Andy onto the dock, a pigmy lifting a giant, and he enjoyed leaning on her while he hopped up the path. "Does it hurt much, darling," she asked.

"No, darling," he answered, with a wink for Jenifer who stopped still and stared.

"Why all the 'darlings'?" Jenifer asked. " 'Yes, darling' and 'no, darling' with 'poor lamb' thrown in?"

"Lacey's a good fisherman," Andy grinned. "She caught me—and how!"

"You don't mean it! Oh, *no!*" Jenifer tried to hug them, both together, then she began to jump up and down and scream, "Cyril, Peter, Alice, everyone! Come quick!"

Andy and Lacey held an announcement party on the path. Jordons rushed down the hill, delirious with excitement. "I think it's the most thrilling thing I ever heard," Jenifer cried. "I'm completely bowled over."

"Well, don't be," Andy said, sagging against Lacey again, "I was—and look what happened to me."

He held out his leg and they all bent down to stare at the hook that was imbedded in the skin beside his shin bone.

"We've got to get him to a hospital," Lacey said, stopping the jokes that were going back and forth. "I don't think any of us should try to get the thing out, do you?"

"No." Peter was positive about it so they sent him off for the car while they made up an excited escort that somehow got Andy up the hill.

"Alice, Gwenn, you two can go with us if you want to," Jenifer motioned, directing the seating arrangement in the car from force of long habit, "but you'll have to sit on the floor. I'll drive and Peter and Cyril can help Andy. The rest of you back up and stay out of the way so I won't run over you."

"*I'll* help Andy," Lacey retorted, "the poor fish belongs to me now."

Somehow they piled in the car and somehow they tore through town without being arrested. When they reached the gate at the entrance to the post a guard saluted Andy and waved them on, and Jenifer pulled up at the curb before a group of frame hospital buildings.

"You aren't *all* going in, are you?" Andy asked in dismay, watching them jump out to surround him.

"Sure," Peter answered. "You'll probably have an anesthetic and they'll have to wheel you. . . ."

"They'll probably shoot in some novocain and yank the darn thing out. I'll be back in five minutes."

"Oh, but Andy," cried Alice, "it won't be any fun if we don't go inside and suffer with you. We want to walk up and down the corridor and wring our hands."

"Oh, for Pete sake." He sighed, then laughed. The Jordons were having their usual enthusiastic time. They stood in the road looking as wistfully at the hospital as at a circus tent and Andy relented. "Come on," he invited half-heartedly, thinking how absurd he must look, hobbling in with such a following, and hoping none of his fellow-fliers would see him. "Let's get going."

It took some time to find the Out Patient Clinic, still longer to find an orderly who could find the Officer of the Day, but after that was done it took no time at all. Andy disappeared into an office and his co-sufferers had hardly seated themselves to listen for groans before he was back again with but a small gauze pad on his leg.

Gwenn pouted with disappointment as she trailed back to the car. "If that's all that happens," she said, "I wish I'd stayed at home and done my arithmetic."

"Well, we might drive by and break the news to Lacey's father," Andy suggested, feeling his operation had not been the success they had anticipated, "about having me for a son-in-law, I mean. You can get a first-hand view of his reaction and can lend me your moral support."

"Let's." Jenifer swung the car around a corner and without waiting for Lacey's consent, trod on the gas throttle. "Let's be old-fashioned about it," she planned. "Andy can ask for Lacey's hand in marriage and we'll all put in a good word for him."

Lacey began to laugh and when they asked her why she only laughed harder. "She's hysterical from joy," Andy explained, happy because her small hand was penned between both of his big ones.

But when they rushed into Mr. Cadwallader's store everyone understood why Lacey had laughed.

Mr. Cadwallader was leaning on his candy case that was worn smooth along its wooden rim from the daily friction of his arms, and he looked over his glasses at Lacey. "Well, daughter," he said without moving, "I see you've finally made up your mind." And then his eyes shifted with a sly twinkle to Andy. "I hope you know what you're in for, son," he warned. "She's purty much of a problem."

He reached a hand across the case and as Andy grasped it his followers stood for the second time in disappointment. Jenifer went behind the counter and looked up at him.

"Oh, Mr. Cadwallader," she said, "you weren't supposed to act like that. Andy was going to ask you if he could marry Lacey and we were going to tell you his good qualities. We were supposed to plead for him."

"He don't need pleadin' for." Mr. Cadwallader took back his hand and ran it through his sparse hair. "I been waitin' a long time to get me as good a son-in-law as Andy. Do you kids think I'm goin' to risk losin' him?" He chuckled, then broke off to look at Gwenn who had pounced on a box of cookies. "Put that down!" he shouted. "Dang it, for an occasion like this I'm goin' to treat you all to bottles of pop and some angelfood cake. Lacey, you go over to the house and get the cake."

But Lacey was behind the counter too. She put her arms around her father and rubbed her cheek against his. "You're sure you won't mind my marrying?" she asked, "not even if Andy's ordered away from here and I have to go with him?"

"Mind? Why in tarnation should I mind?" he asked crossly. "Young folks have to get married and leave home. I left home, your mother . . ." He pushed his glasses higher and blinked rapidly behind them. "It's steamy in here," he said, taking out his handkerchief and turning his back to her.

He fumbled with the handkerchief until Lacey reached out and took off his glasses. She wiped them on her own small square of white linen, then hooked them over his ears again. "There you are, darling," she said. "Now we'll have the party."

She dropped a light kiss on his nose but he only muttered a gruff thanks and leaning on his counter again, looked across at Cyril who was sitting on the frozen foods box. "I reckon you think we're queer folks over here, don't you, son?" he asked, "girls gettin' engaged and everybody drinkin' pop instead of champagne?"

"I think you're quite—quite swell." Cyril answered with a broad smile and looked directly at the old man. "I feel privileged, sir, to be a part of this."

"And you should, you should." Mr. Cadwallader nodded his head sagely. "'Tain't every foreigner that gets to know the real American folks," he said, "Officers like my son-in-law here and girls like Lacey and Jenifer." He stopped and slid open the door in the back of the candy case. "Alice, you an' Gwenn come around here and see if you can find anything that's fit to eat in this mess of pottage. Maybe your teeth and jaws are strong enough to manage some of it. Peter, you go get the pop out of the cooler."

They were very busy in the little store and customers coming in were waited on by Alice or Gwenn while Mr. Cadwallader proudly told them of the engagement.

"This is all impromptu," he would say, plying them with cake, "just to clinch the matter and make Andy feel kind of welcome. I reckon there'll be some bigger shindigs later on."

"Oh goodness, yes." Jenifer always added her speech

and an ice-cold bottle. "We'll have lots of parties and a simply terrific wedding."

Andy had perched himself beside Cyril and he watched Lacey, grinning crookedly and happily until, suddenly, it was late and Jenifer exclaimed:

"Oh, we've got to go home. Ellin will be worried stiff and we'll make Rosie late for the movies." She found Mr. Cadwallader's hat, clapped it on his head and almost pushed everyone out the door. "We'll carry on the celebration at our house," she decided, "with spaghetti and custard pudding."

As they hurried out to the car Andy hung back and kept Lacey with him. "Do you suppose we'll ever be alone?" he asked. "Just to make a few plans of our own?"

"Darling, I doubt it." Lacey tucked her arm through his and reminded him, "You're marrying into a big family, you know."

"Yeah, but so are you," he retorted. "And I'll bet we'll have to live with 'em and love 'em and manage 'em."

"Well, aren't those some of the reasons you gave for marrying me?" Lacey looked up at him and he held her close to him.

"Sure," he answered. "We've got a job cut out for us."

"A big one."

"And when I go back overseas?"

"I'll carry on."

"Good girl." He smiled down at her in the dusk then let out a whoop that brought heads from all the windows in the car. "I'm lucky," he shouted, "and oh gosh, kids, you don't know it—but you're even luckier!"

CHAPTER XIV

BARRY stood at the sunroom window listening to the rain that beat on the shrubbery in a rhythmic accompaniment to the gurgling fountain. Jenifer was curled up on the pink-and-white-striped cushions of a bamboo settee and she watched him lift, then drop the handle on the window, lift and drop, until she could stand it no longer.

"Barry," she asked bluntly, "are you unhappy about Lacey?"

"A little," he answered, without self-consciousness. "But then I've never known anyone quite like Lacey and I've had so little time to enjoy girls that perhaps I'm confusing enjoyment with love."

Behind him Jenifer had to smile. Barry had such a neat mind. It was almost like a desk lined with pigeon holes, one that he sat down to and kept in order, regularly and systematically. Up to now one pigeon hole had been quite empty and he was a little confused by the miscellaneous collection that had to be stuffed under a card marked "Love." She was about to say so for she thought he would understand what she meant when he went on:

"You see, I worked my way through Harvard, and that kept me on the jump, and then Cyril was my first job. I've never been in a position to know girls for I've never had anything to offer them, no prospect of marriage that is, so I've made it a point to be careful of my emotions. Being thrown with Lacey," he left the window and came to sit near her, still intent on his own reasoning, "knowing

Lacey," he said thoughtfully, "has made me realize that I'm very vulnerable. Don't you think so?"

He looked at her so earnestly from behind his thick glasses that Jenifer had difficulty finding the right words for her answer.

"I think that's it, Barry," she said at last. "You aren't really in love, you've only been exposed to it."

"Then I shall have to be more careful." His mouth quirked humorously and he leaned back in his chair with a puff of relief. "Since there are no inoculations against it I don't want to be catching it everywhere I go. It hurts."

"But not for long." Jenifer grinned and tucked her feet under her. "It wears off I hear like a summer cold, until you get bitten by the real bug. Then watch out, for I think you're the kind who will have it hard, like double pneumonia."

They smiled at each other, enjoying her simile, and Jenifer was knowing Barry as she had never had an opportunity to know him, when Mrs. Van Courtlandt bustled in.

"Jenifer," she began without preamble, "I'm at my wit's end. If Cyril is going to start moping again, and sighing, and saying he won't leave Florida that has become hotter than a bake oven, I give up." She threw herself into a chair, and looking at her Jenifer decided she really must be upset, for a strand of hair had escaped from a comb and she paid no attention to it. "He says he won't sit out on Long Island all summer," she went on, "that he's going back to England."

"He can't go back," Jenifer said. "He isn't old enough to enlist yet."

"I told him that, so he said he'd enlist in Canada."

"But they'll find out about him and about the piece of steel fragment in his back and he'll be disappointed and hurt again. Oh, Aunt Kate," Jenifer sat up straight and exclaimed, "we mustn't let him do it."

"Of course we mustn't," Mrs. Van Courtlandt shrugged wearily, "but I can do nothing with him. You're the one who will have to stop him."

"I?"

"Yes, and don't argue about it, Jenifer; you'll have to come to Long Island for the summer."

"Oh, Aunt Kate, I can't." Jenifer slumped back again. "You know I can't. I couldn't possibly leave the children."

"You have Ellin and I'll send another maid over if you need her. Ellin's like a mother to the children."

"But they're my responsibility. And it's not that I wouldn't love to go North where it's cool and have a lovely summer with you and Cyril, but I couldn't leave them."

"Not even if Andy and Lacey would live in the house?"

"Not even then." Jenifer smoothed her skirt over her knees and watched Barry stealing out as noiselessly as a ghost. "I promised Daddy, Aunt Kate, that the children would come before anything else, and they always will. Why, suppose Vance should get the croup as he some-times does! Ellin could take care of him, of course, but he gets so frightened; and Bitsy has bad dreams and has to hold my hand in the night. If I weren't there . . . Oh no," Jenifer shook her head. "Thank you, Aunt Kate, but as much as I'd love to help Cyril, I can't."

Mrs. Van Courtlandt got up and began walking around the room, straightening an ornament on a table, breaking off a dried leaf from the vines around the fountain, while Jenifer watched her. "Will you explain that to Cyril?" she said at last. "I promised him you would come."

"Of course I will. Where is he?"

"Up in his room. I asked him to wait there until I had talked to you."

"Then I'll go up. I'm sorry I can't do as you wish. You've been so good to me and I'd like to help you, but you do understand, don't you?" Jenifer stood up while Mrs. Van Courtlandt went on looking at the vines.

"Yes, my dear, I understand." The answer was unwilling but sincere and Jenifer had to be content with it.

She went up the wide staircase trying not to wonder what a summer on Long Island would be, and hoping she could resist the enticing arguments Cyril would be sure to put up. She feared he might be difficult but when she reached his door he looked up from his desk and the history book he was studying to say:

"So I see you aren't going. I said you wouldn't."

"Oh, Cyril," Jenifer went across the deep thick carpet to the desk and dropped into an upholstered chair beside it, "you're upsetting Aunt Kate again."

"I'm not at all." He closed his book and sat with his hands resting on it. "I merely thought of some things I'd like to do and made the mistake of trying to tell her about them. I didn't mean to be temperamental or difficult but she took it that way. She likes to fuss over me and hasn't had much chance lately, so I suppose she thought this was a good opportunity to fix something for 'the dear boy.'"

"And you didn't sigh and mope?"

"Of course I didn't sigh and mope." Cyril gave the book a shove and rested his elbows on the table. "I stopped that sometime ago," he said, "but I may take it up again if she doesn't let me alone. Aunt Kate is a born manager and I wish you were coming along so she could spend some of her talents on you."

"I wish I could, but Cyril, you understand why I can't, don't you?"

"Yes." He was silent for a moment then asked, "How about letting me take one of the children? I'd look after him."

"You mean . . . will you be there this summer, if I don't go?"

"Of course I'll be there. Aunt Kate was only cooking up a good story and I suppose, had you agreed to go, I would never have had the courage to tell you the difference. I know I'm not ready for the army yet; next year, yes, but Barry says not to try it this summer. So I'd like to have something alive around the place."

"Which one would I send?"

"I don't know. Let's ask Aunt Kate."

They heard Mrs. Van Courtlandt coming up the stairs and when Cyril had broached the plan she took it much better than either he or Jenifer had expected. Peter's name came up first but Jenifer shook her head.

"He wouldn't leave Royal," she said, "and I don't think I could manage without him. And, too, he'd worry about being away as much as I would."

"Then what about Gwenn?" Katherine Van Courtlandt asked.

"She'd never go without Alice, or if she did, poor little Alice would pine away."

"Then let's take them both," Cyril suggested. "They can finish school there and they'll be fun to have around."

"Or Donny." Down in her heart Jenifer was hoping they would invite Donny because he was losing weight. "He isn't as tough, no, not tough, but as hardy as the rest of us," she said, "and I worry about him being down here this summer."

"Then we'll put him on the list too." Cyril had taken the reins into his own hands, as much for Jenifer's sake as his own, and he turned to his aunt and asked, "How about taking all three of them? I'd have a lot of fun showing them around."

"Well, if it will make you happy, dear boy."

There was nothing Katherine Van Courtlandt would not do to make life pleasant for Cyril, and as the children would mean no trouble to her it was settled. Cyril walked home with Jenifer to tell the news to the children, and as they hopped over puddles in the lane he asked, "Jenny, will this make the summer a little easier for you?"

"Oh, lots. With three children out of the way I'll be on vacation."

"And I'll look after them just as you do. It will make me feel as if I'm still with you, to have them to care for and talk with. You know," he looked out at her from under his dripping rain hat and said, "they will be a talisman from you to cherish until fall."

"That's sweet, Cyril."

"And I'll love them, just the way you love them, and the way Alfred loved Lolly and me."

Jenifer thought that after a week or two of them he might change his mind but refrained from saying so and privately determined to give them daily instructions, especially Gwenn, on behaving themselves.

They accepted the news of their visit joyfully and in the days that followed, when everyone was in a mad rush over the wedding that was to be held on the Jordon lawn, insisted on bringing out luggage, drawing lots for the best pieces, and packing and repacking until their treasured possessions were becoming soiled and worn out.

"Gwenn, I've told you a dozen times you cannot have a white fur evening jacket," Jenifer said one Sunday morning, coming into the girls' barracks to find suitcases on the beds and Alice trying to mend an old perfume atomizer.

"But I have plenty of money to buy it and I think you're being very stingy."

Gwenn stood with her head in the air, her hands behind her, and Jenifer looked at her a long time before she answered.

"We might as well get this straight, Gwenn," she said. "I know you have more money than the rest of us, you and Alice. Your first father left you quite a lot."

"A million dollars?"

"No, not a million dollars, but enough that, with Daddy

managing it, it will amount to a great deal by the time you're both grown."

"Half-a-million dollars?"

"Not even that. I don't know exactly, but a lot." Alice had come around the bed and Jenifer explained to them both, "Daddy appointed a Trust Company to take care of it and he only uses a small part of the income each year, just enough for your clothes. It will be expensive to send you up to Aunt Kate's because you'll have to have some new things and there'll be your train fare, so we can't be foolish about it."

"Donny isn't as rich as we are, is he?" Gwenn asked.

"No, he inherited some money too but not as much as you did. I'll buy his things. . . ."

"Alice and I are the richest in the whole family," Gwenn interrupted to toss her head and say airily, "I'll bet I'm as rich as Aunt Kate."

"Oh, Gwenn." Jenifer pushed a suitcase aside and sat down on the bed and Alice squeezed in beside her. "Why do you care how rich you are?" she scolded, putting her arm around Alice who was patting her cheek for attention. "Yes, darling, what is it?"

"Are you rich too?" Alice asked.

"Not that I've heard of." Jenifer laughed and Alice said:

"Then I'll give you half of mine."

"Thanks, pet." She rubbed her cheek against Alice's soft brown hair and Gwenn rushed across the room to throw herself at her feet.

"I will too!" she cried, hugging Jenifer around the waist. "I want you to have pretty things and to swish around and wear diamond rings and white fur jackets." And then she looked up and suggested, "If we had a white fur jacket we could both wear it."

"If we had a white fur jacket," Jenifer laughed, "we'd want a hundred things to go with it. But you *are* going to have a light blue Spring coat."

"I am?" Gwenn's eyes began to sparkle and Jenifer said: "Yes, and I thought Alice could have a red one."

"Oh, boy!"

"And what else, Jenifer?" Gwenn got on her knees and begged. "New slippers?"

"Yes, but with only one stamp apiece you'll have to choose between white or patent leather."

The girls rushed to the closet to drag out their shoes, and looking at the collection they lined up Jenifer thought the display looked pretty hopeless. "We'll have to see the ration board," she decided. "Poor kids, you're going straight through the toes, aren't you?"

Donny's wardrobe was simpler and Ellin was able to manage most of it while Jenifer and Mrs. Van Courtlandt shopped with the girls. Lacey went with them sometimes but her thoughts were on her trousseau and she was apt to see a dress she liked for herself and to disappear into a fitting room.

"There's only one more week to wait," Gwenn cried one afternoon, opening her packages on the kitchen table and showing her purchases to Rosie. "Just think, Rosie, in one more week we'll be on the train!"

And that was the day Alice fell out of the barn loft and broke her collar bone.

Lacey and Andy were in the living room checking the list of wedding guests, and Jenifer and Cyril were painting the boat when they heard the screams. Neal came streaking across the lawn yelling as if the whole Japanese army were after him, and Alice, when they got to the stable, was struggling up out of the scattered hay.

They had to tell her she was brave. Among all the other things they said they had to tell her that. She made no sound while the bone was set and after it was all over she sat on the divan, her arm strapped across her chest, looking rather white and very penitent.

"I didn't mean to go up there," she said to the circle that sat or stood, looking at her. "Peter's always telling us not to climb the ladder because it's rickety, but I wanted to see if any birds . . . I guess I've caused a lot of trouble," she murmured, looking down at her wrinkled dress.

Bits of hay still stuck to her hair and she looked so forlorn that Jenifer went to sit beside her. "It isn't the trouble that matters, darling," Jenifer said, picking out the hay, "it's the suffering for you and having to miss your trip that we mind."

"Do you mean I can't go on the trip?" Alice's big dark eyes looked up, then shot across the room to Gwenn who was sitting on the floor crying. "I can't go to Aunt Kate's?"

"No, and you've kept me from going too," Gwenn sniffled. "You know I can't leave you. I think you were selfish and horrid to be climbing around at the last minute. Everybody's been warning you."

"But I can go, Jenifer," Alice looked up again to plead, "I *feel* all right."

"Darling, you can't dress and undress yourself and you can't eat with your left hand. It wouldn't be fair to Aunt Kate, you know."

"And you might bump your shoulder," Lacey said.

"I'd sit still all the time."

"I have a picture of that." Andy, who was leaning against the mantel, grinned but Cyril slid forward on his chair and clasped his hands around his crossed knee.

"Listen," he said, "I offered to take the kids for the summer and it was a for better or worse proposition. This accident happened before I took over, that's all, and my offer still goes."

"But she can't go all done up in bandages." Peter waved his hand helplessly and then let it seek the solace of his hair. "Gosh, Alice," he frowned, "I'm like Gwenn. I think you should have stayed on the ground."

"Well, she didn't." Cyril had never sat in on one of the Jordons' major conferences before and his pity for the culprit overcame his judgement of her crime. "We have good doctors in New York too," he reminded, "and I'll personally help her scoop up her food. One of the maids can comb her hair and keep her clean." He got up and crossed the room while Alice watched his advance toward the divan hopefully. "Don't you worry," he said, sitting down on its arm and patting the top of her head, since it seemed the only part of her that was safe to touch, "we'll manage it, and whenever you get stuck you can come to me. Will you do that?"

"Oh, yes." Alice let out a deep breath of gratitude before she looked around to see what the verdict of the others would be. Peter looked relieved and Gwenn had stopped crying, but Jenifer still sat in thoughtful silence.

"It's all right, Jenny," Cyril said. "I want her to go."

"Really?"

"The house is so big that half the time Aunt Kate won't know we're in it; and it means keeping the talisman bright and shining. It's a part of it."

"All right then—if Aunt Kate doesn't mind." Jenifer leaned over and kissed Alice's dirty cheek. "Poor baby," she said softly, "you do have such a time."

CHAPTER XV

"IF IT rains," Lacey shouted above the noise of the hammers, "I can't bear it." She looked up at a small cloud that lagged behind some larger ones, making a dark blot on the sky, and held her breath until it moved slowly on.

"It won't rain." Andy had his blouse off and he and Peter were down on the grass building a trellis. As a piece was finished he shoved it over to Cyril who painted it white. Cyril, in turn, carried it to Jenifer and Mr. Cadwallader, who propped it upright among a cluster of flowering shrubs that had been transplanted that morning. Eventually the trellis would be trimmed with smilax and Easter lilies, for Lacey and Andy were to be married before it.

Mrs. Van Courtlandt's gardener had superintended the transplanting, and because he worked so surely and expertly Jenifer had a faint hope that the shrubs would live and bloom again as a reminder of this beautiful day.

"Sugar, stop fretting," Andy comforted Lacey. "If it rains we'll pick up the whole shebang and set it up inside. We can be married just as legally indoors as out."

"But not as artistically." Lacey went on rushing about, getting in everyone's way. She ran into the house and out again, checked this and rechecked that, until her father stopped trying to brace a piece of the trellis Jenifer was holding upright and said:

"Daughter, you're going to be plum worn out. Why don't you sit over there by Alice and keep still."

"I can't, I'm too excited," Lacey cried. But she did sit down on the grass and Andy left his pounding to come over and drop a kiss on her hot cheek.

"You aren't running a fever, are you?" he asked anxiously.

"Heavens, no, but pretty soon it's going to be four o'clock and people will arrive."

"Then I'll put on my blouse and you can tuck your shirt-tail back in your shorts and we'll stand up and get married whether your father has time to get out from under the dinkus or not."

But Lacey jumped up. "I forgot to tell Ellin that I want to use my grandmother's silver punch bowl!"

"The bowl was polished last week," Jenifer laughed, rubbing paint from her hands with a turpentined rag. "It has ice in it and is ready to be filled and carried out to the table."

"Oh." Lacey was meek as she sat down again, and Alice fished a piece of gum from her pocket.

"Chew this," she advised. "It helps."

Lacey said "thank you" absently but forgot to unwrap the gum for Gwenn called from the side porch:

"The slips to the bridesmaids' dresses didn't come. I've looked everywhere for them."

"Oh dear." She was off like a track runner and Alice said eagerly:

"Andy, the slips are in the boys' closet, shall I go find them?"

"Lord, no. Stay where you are and don't break again.

With your arm unhooked so you can be in the wedding anything can happen to you."

So Alice sat still and watched the activity around her, and the sky cleared until by sun-time it was three o'clock.

"Boy, does Royal shine!" Peter gloated, giving Royal one last rub even though Jenifer had called him in to dress.

"And Timothy Two's not so bad. They're a good match for each other." Cyril had tied his bay thoroughbred in the stable runway ready for his part in the ceremony, and as they hurried out Peter called:

"When it's time you snatch up Grandfather's Civil War saber and I'll take Dad's."

"Right. I'll see you in an hour."

Cyril ran for home and Peter went inside to what he considered a lunatic asylum. Two girls who looked like Gwenn and Alice, only older and much prettier, were dancing through the halls in long diaphanous yellow dresses that swished along the floor. A small one that should have been Bitsy sat like a pink statue on a chair, holding a basket of rose petals, her face completely hidden behind a large tulle bow on the basket but patiently not minding. Another one, dressed in blue and with a crop of curls instead of stubby pigtails, could have passed for Susan except that she too sat. Peter had never seen such docility and he looked twice before he grinned.

"You'd better hurry, son," a voice called. "Danged if I think I'm goin' to last it out."

Peter stopped at the living room door and looked in at

Mr. Cadwallader. He was almost as stiff as the two figures in the hall except that his bow tie had slipped a little and he held an empty pipe between his teeth. "Gettin' married is a chore," he said. "Have you seen the groom around?"

"Not lately, but I suppose he'll show up."

"Could be that he's out wirin' up that lily that worried Lacey." Mr. Cadwallader got up, put his pipe in his pocket and squeaked to the window, then shook his head. "Nope. And the lily's still saggin' a little. I reckon I'll slip out and fix it."

"Father, don't go away." Lacey stood in the door and the old man turned to look at her.

She wore her white net wedding dress, the small round collar only a very little whiter than her throat, her hair blue-black under a cloud of white tulle that cascaded down and was looped over her arm. Mr. Cadwallader blinked at her, then held out his arms and Lacey rushed into them.

"It's almost time!" Jenifer cried, floating in like a foamy green wave. "Is Peter dressing?"

"I d'know, he was here a minute ago." Mr. Cadwallader released Lacey and set to work polishing his glasses.

"Then he must be nearly ready." Jenifer took her place at the window, careful not to be seen, and exclaimed joyfully, "Simply loads of people are pouring in and Aunt Kate is doing a marvelous job of receiving them, but you should be out there too."

"Of course you should, Father." Lacey gave him a push and he muttered as he squeaked dutifully out:

"Well, dang it, how'm I goin' to know when to come and get you?"

"You'll know." Jenifer pointed to a harp and some violins under the trees. "Before Peter tells the orchestra to start playing the Wedding March he'll hunt you up and you can come to the side porch. Lacey will be in the door, all ready." They watched him go out onto the lawn and Lacey smiled proudly at the friendly way he spoke to his guests.

"Are we all here?" she asked nervously. "Are the boys outside and has anyone found Andy?"

"Donny's hunting him." Jenifer sighed, her eyes searching through the crowd on the lawn. "Grooms are so unpredictable," she worried. "They get nervous and then there's no telling what they'll do. And Barry's no help as best man." She risked being seen to lean close to the screen and to say, "There comes Donny, and from the way he's looking around and staring at everyone he hasn't found him."

"Oh, my goodness!" Gwenn was tired of twirling around in her daffodil skirt and what they were saying filtered through to her. She clapped her hand over her mouth and looked at them round-eyed above it. "I forgot to tell you. Barry left the ring at home and he and Andy went back for it."

"Then I must tell Ellin to go out and hold the music." Jenifer whisked out of the room, calling back, "Alice, stand at the window and watch for them. When you see them coming, whistle or. . . ."

"They're here! Hold everything," Alice shouted. "Andy's

mopping his forehead and making some kind of signal to go ahead."

"Then line up and I'll start you." Jenifer was back and leading Bitsy. "Susan, you go first," she said, "and remember to walk slowly. Just step, hold, step, like we practised. Gwenn, you and Alice keep right together, and Alice hold your flowers higher on your chest so your arm will protect your shoulder. Bitsy, you follow me and be sure to scatter your petals in front of Lacey. Now be ready, all of you."

The music began to play softly and there were gasps of admiration as the Jordon girls came slowly across the lawn. Andy, standing at the trellis, watched them come toward him with a heartful of pride until he lifted his eyes to the porch and saw Lacey. Then only Barry's restraining hand kept him from going to meet her.

"Dearly beloved, we are gathered here," the chaplain said, just as the sun came out. It shone on the bowed heads, disappeared for a moment like a solemn benediction, and when the chaplain finished his farewell words it blazed out gaily with the orchestra, as Lieutenant and Mrs. Andrew Compton turned to greet their guests.

"It was beautiful!" Jenifer cried, clinging to Lacey. "It was perfect, so just relax and have a good time. The rest will go off just as well."

She scattered the children, saw that Gwenn was clinging faithfully to Alice, then found Cyril and went off with him to look at the bride's table. It was set on the lawn above the lake and was garlanded with smilax that had gardenias studded through it. The towering white cake stood at one end, the silver punch bowl filled with lime sherbet at the other, and mints and nuts in silver dishes were scattered over the lace cloth. The lawn was dotted with tables and chairs and the Van Courtlandt maids were carrying out plates of chicken salad and rolls.

"Doesn't it look lovely?" she said. "I've never been this close to a wedding before and I wish we could have one every day."

"I don't." Cyril stood by the table but his eyes were on Jenifer. He wished he dared suggest that they go down to sit on the A. CADWALLADER bench but he only said, "I'm dizzy from rushing around so fast and keep hoping no one will bump into the fresh paint."

Jenifer laughed. "You would be practical at a time like this. And now we must mingle around and see that everyone is served."

The reception was over. Guests were drifting toward the front lawn, waiting for Lacey to appear in her traveling dress. Andy's light summer uniform needed no changing so he checked the luggage in her coupe that stood just outside the gates, hoping that when the time came he could maneuver it through the dozens of other cars that were parked in the lane. He grinned at the old shoes and tin cans tied on behind and felt in his pocket to be sure his good strong knife was there. Then Vance ran out for him and he went inside to tell Lacey's father good-by.

Lacey was in the hall too, in a pale gray suit with a bunch of blue flowers and a short saucy veil on her head and Andy wanted to look at her and no one else. But the Jordons were clinging to him and Mr. Cadwallader was pumping his hand, so he grinned and said anything that came into his head, and none of it made good sense to him but made everyone else laugh or cry.

"Come on, you two," Jenifer said. "Cyril and Peter are ready."

Someone shoved Lacey's hand into Andy's, the screen door flew open, and as they stepped out onto the small portico, Peter and Cyril, on their horses at the bottom of the steps, lifted their sabers to form an arch.

Lacey and Andy went down the steps and under the arch, and although it was unrehearsed, the Jordons poured after them. Paper rose petals fluttered through the air like a pink snow storm and Cyril and Peter, warily circling the crowd, took up their station in front of the car.

"Good-by, good-by," everyone called as Andy held open the door for Lacey. She waved through the window, Andy stopped in the road to shake his own hands above his head in self-congratulation, then the motor roared. Royal pranced a little at the sound and Timothy Two tried to imitate him until Andy let out the clutch. The car rolled slowly along the lane, its military escort trotting briskly in front, and those on the lawn released a deep sigh of pleasure.

"Wasn't it the most divine wedding?" Jenifer said to Mr. Cadwallader who was ensconced in a chair in the living room with children at his feet, on the chair's arms, and hanging over its back.

He had his coat off and wore a pair of Peter's bedroom slippers, and because he had been too excited to eat before, Ellin had brought him his supper on a tray.

"Where do you think they'll go on their trip?" Gwenn

asked, jumping up to turn on the lamp beside him. "To Daytona?"

"They've got more gas than that," he chuckled, trying to keep Susan's new curls out of his chicken salad. "Andy's got ten days' leave, with a gallon a day for it, and Lacey's might nigh walked us both to death, savin' up. 'Twouldn't surprise me if they get clear to Miami."

"That would be wonderful! And you'll stay with us until they come back, won't you?" Jenifer had brought a footstool for his feet and she propped them up on it and sat down beside them.

"Why in tarnation should I?"

"So you won't be lonely."

"Shucks, I never get lonely." He took a bite of salad and popped a piece of roll into Bitsy's open pink mouth. "I've got a lot to do around home, getting ready for my new son to move in." He let his eyes rove over the room, thinking of his own boy who had lived in this little house, and Jenifer said quickly:

"Run and take your party dresses off, children. We have to pack the rest of Gwenn's and Alice's clothes tonight. And Neal," she called, "hang up that white suit carefully. It has to last you all summer."

There was confusion in the house again. Girls who had been grownup young ladies for a few hours, ran around in shorts, and from his chair in the living room Mr. Cadwallader inspected new shoes, and admired hair ribbons and lapel pins, and even Donny's new underwear. But at last it was nine o'clock and he stood up to go.

"You're sure, darling, you won't be lonely?" Jenifer

asked in the hall, her arms around him while Peter went for the car.

"Dang it, no," he answered with his usual brusque independence. "I'm no flibberty-jibbert who minds his daughter goin' off on a little trip. I'm a lucky man, Jenifer."

"You are, you really are." Jenifer drew his head down to kiss him. "And you're a dear man and I love you."

"Well, I love you too, dang it," he growled, pushing her away and shuffling out the door, still in Peter's slippers, "but you stop that packin' and get to bed early."

"I will." Jenifer let the screen door close slowly and stood until she heard the car drive off. Then she went back to the girls' barracks and looked around at the disorder.

"I don't see how I can bear to have you go tomorrow," she sighed, sitting down on a bed and folding a slip of Gwenn's. She laid the slip on her knee and sat smoothing it while Gwenn and Alice ran over to cuddle close to her.

"You won't worry about us, will you?" Alice asked.

"No, I won't worry but I'll miss you so much. We've never been separated before, and while I know it's a wonderful opportunity and Daddy would want you to have it, still. . . ."

"But we'll be back soon and if we get homesick we'll come right home."

"I wouldn't want you to do that," Jenifer began, when to her surprise Gwenn spilled onto the floor and buried her face in her lap. "I c-can't go, J-Jenifer," she sobbed, "not even to have a butler wait on me and a m-maid of my own maybe, and to see the Empire State building and perhaps a night club. I c-can't leave you."

"Why, lamb!" Jenifer laughed heartily in spite of her joy at Gwenn's sincere little demonstration. If Alice had cried she would have understood, but for *Gwenn* to cry! She jumped up from the bed, toppling Gwenn in a heap, and urged, "Let's rush through this mess and stop being sentimental ninnies. I think it's swell that you're going. We're all just a little on the weepy side from the wedding. So let's get to work, men, dang it."

CHAPTER XVI

JENIFER ran down the front steps and waved a letter at Cyril who was turning in the gate on Timothy Two. She wore her jodhpurs and went leaping across the lawn in long strides. "I've had a letter from Daddy," she cried, "and he's been in England on a trip, and guess what?"

"He saw Mum and Father."

"Yes!"

"Well, get Royal and you can tell me about it while we ride along."

"All right, I'll hurry." Jenifer dragged Royal out of his stall where he had been resting from the wedding, and said to Cyril as he buckled the saddle girth, "Are you sure we have time for a ride this morning?"

"The train leaves at two-something and Paul will take the bags down early so there's no hurry. Mount up."

So Jenifer swung herself into the saddle and they rode slowly through the yard and down the lane.

"Doing things for the last time is sad, isn't it?" she said when they passed the vacant lot where they had exchanged so many confidences under the live oak tree.

"Not when it isn't forever. I'll be back in the fall and we'll do everything over again. Suppose we jog around Mr. Peterson's citrus groves and then come back here and you can read me your father's letter?"

"Here, or on the A. CADWALLADER bench?"

"Here. It's quiet and no kids."

"All right." Jenifer pushed Royal into a trot and then an easy canter.

It was warm in the early morning sunshine and after they had made the circuit she mopped her face and pulled her shirt loose from her hot back while she watched Cyril tie the horses to a scrub pine. His dark hair that was almost as short as Peter's now, curled damply and he was brown under the open V of his shirt. He threw himself on the ground under the tree and Jenifer sat down beside him, her knees hunched up, her arms clasped around them.

"Now, let's hear what your father has to say," he invited, comfortable, with his head resting on a root.

Jenifer took the letter from her pocket slowly. "Doesn't it seem strange," she asked, "to think that Daddy knows more about you and your family than I do? That he's seen your parents and your home?"

"He has? Oh, I say!" Cyril raised himself on one elbow while Jenifer began to read the letter.

"He says, 'I had a charming note from Lady Carlington in answer to mine, saying they were unable to come up to London and urging me to spend a week-end with them. So I took a few hours off and it was well worth it. She is a lovely little person.'" Here Jenifer's eyes dropped down a few lines for her father had written, "and it is difficult to realize that she is crippled and will never walk again. It seems that Cyril has been kept in ignorance of this so I trust you not to mention it."

"'Lord Carlington,'" she went on, "'is a man after my own heart. We talked war and politics and about you children. He is very proud of Cyril and is looking forward to the day when he will come home.'"

"You see?" she said, "how silly you were to think your father was disappointed in you?"

"Yes," he muttered, trying not to look too pleased, "but go on."

" 'Their house, or rather their castle, for it is a castle, is one of the most beautiful I have seen. Built in sixteen-hundred-and-something, it has all the towers and secret stairways that would thrill you, plus what I enjoyed (and what is due to Lady Carlington being an American, no doubt) excellent heat and plumbing.' " Both Cyril and Jenifer laughed at that and Cyril said:

"Mum did insist on that. She put bathrooms all over the place."

"And furnaces?"

"Oh, scads of furnaces. We nearly melt."

"Cyril," Jenifer laid the letter on her knee and said thoughtfully, "you didn't tell me that your father, and then you, someday, would be the Earl of Easterbrook."

"I didn't think of it. Grandfather's a hale old man. And Jenny, titles have come to mean nothing to me since I've been over here—unless you earn them, titles like General, such as your father has. I'd give any I may ever have to be called Lieutenant, like Andy."

"You will be." Jenifer sat smoothing the letter absently. "I'm kind of jealous of Daddy," she said slowly, "for knowing your mother and father and seeing your home. I feel sort of . . . sort of left out."

"But you'll come over to visit us someday." Cyril rolled over on his stomach and looked up at her. "Will you come, Jenny?" he asked. "When the war is over?"

"I'd love to."

"And I'll show you everything."

"The pear vine?"

"The pear vine and the horses and the gardens, and Mum will take us up to London to dine in whatever places are left, and I'll show you my secret room where I used to play I was a knight and slept on the floor."

"And caught cold, I'll bet."

"Sniffled like the dickens. Would you like that, Jenny?"

"Oh, I'd adore it."

"Then we'll plan on it. And look, I've got a couple more talismans for us. They're just some things I picked up in a shop but they'll work for us." He took two small round glass cases from his pocket and held them in the palm of his hand. They were of double thickness, flat and gold-rimmed, and each had a four-leaf clover inside. "Take one," he said, "and make a wish and always keep the clover near you, and it will work."

Jenifer took one of the cases and held it between her thumb and finger in the light. "We must close our eyes and wish, and we must never tell what we wished."

They sat in silence for a few minutes, each wondering what favor the other was asking, until Cyril burst out, "Did your wish have anything to do with me?"

"Some. Did yours, with me?"

"A lot."

They looked shyly at each other until Jenifer put the little talisman in her shirt pocket and asked a bit self-consciously, "Shall I finish reading the letter now?"

"Not unless you want to. Do you?"

"Not particularly. There isn't much more in it, except one thing."

"What's that?"

"Something that has a little to do with my wish." She dropped her knees and tucked her feet under her, and leaning over to part the grass and push it back together again, said, "Do you remember the day I was afraid I had failed? The day I fainted?"

"Yes."

He nodded and she went on without looking up, "Well, I wrote to Daddy about it. It takes such a long time to get an answer and I just had it today. He thinks I'm doing all right."

"But you knew you were."

"I didn't quite know. Sometimes I thought so and then something would come up that I should do and I'd say to myself, 'oh, I'm just too tired,' and so. . . ."

"And so you'd do it."

"Not always. Sometimes I let things slide. But Daddy says he's proud of me, just like your father, and I feel happier about it."

She looked up then and Cyril reached out to take her hand from the grass. "Jenny," he said, holding it in both of his, "there isn't a girl in a million who would give up a trip to New York. I wish you weren't so conscientious."

"I do too."

She chuckled at her own frankness, the nearest she had come to telling how hard it had been for her to give up the trip, then got to her feet. Cyril still held her hand and he kept it as they walked to the horses. He untied them and helped her to mount, and as he swung himself into the saddle she gathered up her reins and said:

"Good-by, Cyril."

"Good-by, Jenny." He reached across to her and both horses stood quite still while he kissed her, then went walking out to the lane.

The house was in utter confusion when Jenifer gave Royal a slap that sent him to the stable alone. Donny stood dejectedly in the hall holding a pair of tennis shoes Ellin had forgotten to pack, Vance and Bitsy, without naps, were chasing each other from room to room, the remains of lunch were still on the table and Peter was eating alone.

"This is a fine time to come home," he put down his fork to say. "The kids have more stuff left out than they've packed."

"Then hunt up another suitcase." Jenifer snatched a jelly sandwich and ran along the hall to the girls' room. Ellin was there and Alice sat on a chair, her arm strapped again, and perspiring in her new red coat.

"My goodness, what have you got that on for?" Jenifer cried, helping her out of it.

"Gwenn said we should be dignified and wear them."

"Well, I notice she isn't done up for the Arctic." Jenifer looked at Gwenn who was at the dresser trying on her new blue felt beanie.

"It's just because I haven't got that far," Gwenn answered haughtily. "I had to dress Alice first."

"Sure, and it's a big hilp ye were." Ellin was putting the

room to rights and she looked severely at Gwenn. "Talkin'
about how ye're goin' to ride in a drawin' room and tip
the porter and have iced tea sint in, while I put the poor
child's dress on. 'Tis a good mind I have to keep ye at
home."

She winked at Jenifer, who returned the wink before
she rushed out to settle poor little Donny's troubles.

"Darling, you won't be homesick, will you?" she asked,
stuffing the tennis shoes into a small cardboard suitcase of
books, nails, glue and bits of wood that he insisted on
carrying with him.

"Oh no," he answered, "not with Cyril there. You know,
I'm going to be just like Cyril when I grow up."

"You are?" Jenifer pushed him down on the suitcase so
she could close it. "Rather than like Peter or Andy?" she
asked, sucking her thumb that had got caught in the clasp.

"Sure. We're going to paint together this summer and
he says I can ride with him. Peter and I can't ever ride together because we only have one horse."

There was such hero worship in his eyes as he sat on
the case looking up that Jenifer threw her arms around
him. "Good for you," she said, grinning broadly. "You
stick to that and you'll be a man among men."

At last they were ready to leave for the station. The car
was in the drive, Royal had been wept over, and Rollo
was shut in the kitchen, where he spent most of his days
due to an incurable habit of barking, and Jenifer lined up
the three travelers in the hall for a few last words of
advice.

"Remember," she said, standing before the screen door and surveying them, "you're a soldier's children. You're 'army brats.' And don't you do anything, ever, that will reflect discredit on that soldier or will make the army ashamed to have you as a part of it. Will you remember that?"

"Yes, Jenifer."

"Then think of it the first thing in the morning and the last thing at night. Say to yourselves, 'We'll be good soldiers, too.' Dismissed."

They ran to hug her and only the fact that the lock on the screen door held saved them all. "Listen," she said. "I hear Paul blowing the car horn and that means that the Van Courtlandts are starting." She pressed her lips firmly together and gave them one last hug before she went to get her hat.

She dreaded the good-bys at the station, but when they reached it the train was already coming in and there were but a few moments in which to get the children settled. At the last second she found she was standing on the ground still clutching a red coat and a blue one, and Cyril had to reach down for them. The train began to move, Mrs. Van Courtlandt's handkerchief fluttered from the drawing room she occupied alone, three sad excited faces pressed against a window, and Cyril, looking over the porter's shoulder in the vestibule, saw the little line of Jordons beside the tracks.

He saw them all as the train moved along: Bitsy, Neal, Vance, Susan, Peter. And looking out at them he knew he would always see them, the little Jordons, as an obbligato in a concerto, as the background in a painting. For him, the motif, the lovely figure in the foreground was, and always would be, just Jenifer.